Only If We Could Last

A Desi Girl in a Korean World

KRITIKA SHARMA

BOOKS BY KRITIKA SHARMA

FICTION:

Only If We Could Last

As We Went To Bed

The Rogue Spy – The Delhi Chapter (Book 1)

Desires Series
Treacherous Desires (Book 1)
Desires Revisited (Book 2)

Ghost Series
Live-in with a Ghost (Book 1)
In Love with a Ghost (Book 2)
Forever with a Ghost (Book 3)

Jab We Quarantined (Short Read)
Be My Quarantine (Short Read)

The Slut Chronicles Series:
Betrayed (Book 1)
Enslaved (Book 2)
Obsessed (Book 3)

Perfect Crimes Series:
The Girl Who Died: Perfect Crimes Episode 1
The Stolen Diamonds: Perfect Crimes Episode 2
The Silent Death: Perfect Crimes Episode 3

NON-FICTION:

Manage your Manager

Only If We Could Last

A Desi Girl in a Korean World

(Book 1 of Language of Love Duology)

KRITIKA SHARMA

KALAMOS LITERARY SERVICES LLP

Kalamos Literary Services LLP
Email: info@kalamos.co.in | editorial@kalamos.co.in

First Published in 2025
by
Kalamos Literary Services

ISBN- 978-93- 7349-468-5

Only If We Could Last
Kritika Sharma

Cover designed & typeset in Kalamos Literary Services LLP

Print and bound in India.

For you:

Who still believe in stolen glances, whispered confessions,
and the unspoken language of love.
Come, let's fall in love together.

For you:

Who keeps choosing love, even after it breaks you…
Who still pauses at love songs that quietly take you…
Who always believed it would never last…

Come, let's begin something that will steal your heart.

1

Wah-tuh & Worries

I closed my eyes and exhaled heavily, trying incredibly hard not to fall apart again. I was so upset today that, for the first time, I didn't even realize when the flight took off.

I sniffed and jumped in my seat as the man sitting next to me nudged me lightly. When I turned to him, I realized he was pointing at the air hostess, who was gesturing at me from her seat, signalling to straighten mine. She, too, was strapped in.

I nodded, adjusted my seat, and looked out the window. The plane soared higher, breaking through the clouds. The pilot switched off the 'fasten seatbelt' sign, and I leaned back again.

"Umm, Miss–" the air hostess approached me hesitantly. "Are you alright?"

"I'm fine," I grunted, my throat too choked to say anything more, and simply nodded.

Silently, she handed me two bottles of water before walking away.

I am Somasundaripriya Vibhuti Narayan. Yep, that's my name. A mouthful, isn't it? And it is a whole other story. And since most people – including myself – can't seem to pronounce it correctly, I go by Priya.

"*I hab trabbelled a rot, you no, but I hab neber been accompaneed by a sobbing gurl,*" a man beside me spoke in a distinct, noticeable accent. At least, that's what it sounded like to me!

I blinked and looked at him. He wasn't much older than me and had a kind smile on his face.

"Why don' chu dringk some wah-tuh?" he said, still smiling.

"What?" I asked, confused.

"Wah-tuh," he pointed at the water bottle in my hand, and I finally understood, he meant 'Water'!

Oh, damn. This is my life now, isn't it? I sighed inwardly, taking a sip.

"What did you say before?" I asked, serious now.

He thought for a moment and repeated his sentence.

"Did you mean, 'You have travelled a lot, but you've never been accompanied by a sobbing girl?'" I clarified.

"Weh-r, yesh, I deed. Wha dee-ju heer?" he asked, a slight crease forming on his forehead.

Guessing he had said, 'Yes, I did. What did you hear?' I waved a hand airily. "Never mind." I mean, what could I tell him? That even though he was speaking English, I was too thick to understand his accent?

"I am Ahn Changho. And yoh?" he asked, extending a hand.

"I'm Priya," I said, shaking it.

His smile broadened at this.

"What?" I asked, perplexed.

"Wee Sau-thu Ko-ree-ans ahr-ways in-tro-duse our-selves weeth poo-ru names," he said.

I deciphered most of his sentence, 'We South Koreans always introduce ourselves with *pooru* names.'

"What do you mean by 'pooru names'?" I asked, frowning.

He laughed, shaking his head. "Not pooru, poo-ru, like Ahn Changho, my poo-ru name."

"Ahh, full name," I nodded in understanding.

"Yehs," he said, his eyes crinkling with amusement.

"In South Korea, you put the last name first, right?" I asked, finally warming up to the conversation.

"Yehs," he nodded again.

"So, Ahn is your family name, and Changho is your first name?" I asked, relieved that I'd managed to remember his name correctly.

"Deht ees kuh-rehk," he said, grinning even wider.

"You lost me at the last word," I admitted.

"Kuh-rehk," he repeated, this time more slowly.

But it still went over my head.

I shook my head, still confused, so he pulled out a small diary and scribbled, 'That is correct.'

"Damn it!" I burst into laughter.

He chuckled too before scribbling something else. For the first time since the flight took off, I felt a little lighter.

"For how long you are going to be in South Korea?" he had written.

"Three months," I sighed.

He raised his eyebrows before speaking again.

"Dehn mai dee-ah, yoo ah een truh-buh-ru. Bih-kawz mo-suh peep-ul hav wuh-rse ahk-sehnt den ahy doo," he said, shaking his head.

"Once more, please… and slowly," I requested.

This time, I caught most of it, 'Then, my dear, you are in trouble because most people have a worse accent than I do.'

I repeated it back to him, and he nodded in approval.

"But I do understand why I'm in trouble. People won't slow down for me, and I won't understand a word," I whispered.

"Yehs," he nodded. *"Poh tree muhns,"* he said, raising three fingers.

"I'm doomed," I sighed as I seriously didn't understand whatever he just said, though I guessed it was three months!

"Naht doomd, juhst…" he trailed off, shrugging.

The gesture said it all… I was epically, royally screwed.

2

No Choice, No Escape

Fifteen Days Ago

"Priya, come in here!" Mr. Ashok Tyagi's voice boomed across the office.

I groaned. It was ten minutes to six… almost freedom.

"Come now, Priya," he gestured for me to hurry. Standing at his office door, holding it open, he looked serious.

I sighed, grabbing my things as if that would make a difference. As if I had a choice.

"Please, sit."

I clenched my teeth, resisting the urge to groan again. If my boss was telling me to sit, it was never good news.

"I am not working this weekend," I declared pre-emptively.

Ashok sighed, shaking his head. "It's not about this weekend."

I narrowed my eyes. Not a good sign.

"How long have you worked for me?" he asked, leaning back in his chair.

"Oh my God, it's that bad!" I blurted. My heart rate spiked. "Are you firing me?"

"No, not firing you," he looked genuinely appalled. "Priya, you're my best coder. Hell, you're the best coder in the entire company! How could I fire you?"

Relief washed over me. "Then…?"

"Just answer the question," he pressed.

I eyed him warily. "Eleven years."

"Yes. Eleven years, and in that time, you've risen from intern to head programmer," he nodded, his voice laced with pride.

And yet… something was off.

His usual eye crinkle – the one that always appeared when he was truly happy – was missing.

I folded my arms, "What's going on, Ashok?"

He exhaled sharply, "Fine! Nothing gets past you, does it?"

"If you've known me for eleven years, I've known you just as long," I countered. "You were my boss back then too, remember?"

Back when I was an intern, he was a project manager. And today, well, I was the head programmer of the entire company, and he was, somehow, still my boss!

"Priya…" he hesitated. "I know you have family issues."

"My children are not 'issues,' Ashok! How many times!" I snapped.

"You're almost thirty-two," he shot back, clearly frustrated.

Oh, not this again. "Yes, Ashok. I'm aware of my age. What does that have to do with me sitting in your office at…" I quickly checked my watch, "at 5:57 PM?"

He ignored me, "And you have a twelve-year-old son."

I sighed, "Yes. Rohan. And an eleven-year-old daughter, Dhara. And a ten-year-old son, Dhruv." I tilted my head. "So?"

"You love making your life complicated, don't you?" he shook his head.

"They are my kids, Ashok. And I love them," I stated firmly. I didn't think my adding 'they don't make my life complicated' will change the tone of the conversation.

His expression hardened. "Why did you adopt them at such a young age?"

"That's my decision," I said, voice sharp. "And no matter what happens, I won't give them up."

This wasn't our first argument about it.

I knew he didn't understand my choices, but I also didn't care. My kids were my family. My whole world. And who the hell was he to ask me about them again and again, as if they were his burden! Not that I consider my kids of any kind of burden…

He studied me for a long moment. Then, finally, he exhaled in defeat.

"You're going to Seoul for three months," his voice was clipped. "It's not negotiable. So, prepare your…" he made air quotes, "'family.' And be ready."

My jaw dropped.

"Seoul, as in South Korea?" I asked, unable to believe my ears.

"Yes," he nodded, shuffling through some papers.

"For three months? Why?" I demanded.

"As you know, this is a South Korean company," he started in a crisp tone.

"I know I work for a South Korean company," I snapped.

He paused at my tone before speaking again. "ZenTel is the leading mobile company in the world."

"I know that. If you have forgotten, I personally modify their codes to make their mobiles suitable for the Indian population, making ZenTel top mobile company in India too," I hissed.

"Yes, and now they want these hands in Seoul," Ashok finished pointing at me.

"But I can't. It's exam time. My kids need to study," I argued.

"Your sister takes care of your kids, doesn't she?" he countered.

Yes, my sister, Dhriti and I were raising the kids together, and we had our roles clearly defined. She managed everything at home while I focused on work. She was the caregiver, and I was the breadwinner.

"But I can't go for three whole months," I insisted, standing up.

"ZenTel is developing a new technology, and it is highly classified. They won't share the codes or any details over calls or networks. They need you there, in person, to work with their head developer. They've also called someone from the Europe division. The three of you will work together and deploy it by June this year," Ashok explained.

"I cannot go," I stressed.

"There is money involved, Priya," Ashok said, his voice serious.

I looked at him, appalled. Yes, raising three kids on a single salary in Delhi was tough. We barely got by. But how could he say that?

"The normal stipend per day is 5k, but considering how much they want you there, they have agreed to double it. You will be paid 10k per day for three months," Ashok revealed with a small smile.

I did a quick mental calculation. Assuming 65 working days, that meant 6.5 lakh rupees.

"I already make enough. Why would I need 6-7 lakh rupees if it means living away from my family?" I asked seriously.

"Umm, it's actually 90 days, so 9 lakh rupees, and it's on top of your salary. Your salary will continue while you're in Seoul, plus the stipend. Your stay will be company-paid, your breakfast and dinner covered since you'll be in a company guesthouse. Travel to and from Seoul? Also covered. Basically, you'll only spend on lunch, shopping, and a bit of leisure. So, out of that 9 lakhs, you'll easily save 6-7 lakhs. Imagine the support that money could provide your family," he urged.

I was stunned.

Before I could respond, he added, "If you refuse, they will fire you, Priya. Believe me, they will. And while I'm sure you'd get hired anywhere, do you really want to risk it? Not every manager would be as accommodating as I am, letting their head programmer leave office sharp at 6 while everyone else burns the midnight oil."

And he was right.

"Your visa and tickets," he said, pushing them towards me.

I was shocked.

"I didn't want to alarm you before your visa was approved, so I took the liberty of filing it for you," he admitted with a knowing smile.

"Do they even speak English there?" I asked sceptically.

"Yes, they do. Seoul has a wide population of English speakers, Priya," he sighed.

"And would I understand them?" I asked, well aware of how I often struggled to understand programmers over calls.

"You would. Have you not watched Korean shows? They're trending these days," Ashok laughed.

"They are translated, Ashok," I mocked. "I am sure the accent won't be so smooth."

"Well, I love those shows, and I think of Korean as the language of love. And who doesn't understand love?" he said knowingly.

I grimaced at the thought of 'love'. Who the hell wanted love when it always came with strings attached?

"If I choose to go, I wouldn't see my family for three whole months?" I asked, pushing aside my thoughts.

"I can arrange one additional round trip for a weekend in between," Ashok offered.

"I can't be away from my family for forty-five days, Ashok," I shrieked. "Money be damned! If you think I'll stay away from my family for forty-five days, then meet them only for a weekend, you're crazy. I'd rather test my luck somewhere else."

Ashok's mouth thinned at my words.

"What is your proposal?" he demanded. "You're going, Priya. That's not up for debate. So, what are your conditions?"

I thought for a long moment. I knew if I asked my family, it would be chaos. This was my decision to make. The money could be critical for my family. I could save it for college, or get a term insurance policy so that my kids would be secure if anything happened to me.

"Five-day workweek, right?" I asked seriously.

"Yes, same as here," Ashok nodded.

"Fine. I'll work ten days straight, including weekends, then return home for four days, then go back," I proposed.

Ashok frowned.

"You're asking for six round trips?" he asked, calculating quickly.

"Yes. That way, I can be with my children for four days at a time," I explained.

"I don't think that will be permitted. It will be expensive. Not to mention, how will you work ten days straight and then travel?" he asked, clearly sceptical.

"You leave work to me. Have I ever given you a reason to complain about my work?" I challenged.

Before he could answer, I added, "Find a way to make it work, with my six trips and 10k stipend per day, then we have a deal."

"No stipend for the days you're in India," he warned.

"I know," I nodded, and without another word, I turned and left.

3

Lost without subtitles

Present Day, in Korea...

It was almost a seven-hour flight, and it was one of the most difficult ones. This was my third time on a plane and my first international trip. I couldn't believe that I would be traveling for eleven more times in the next three months.

And why was this flight so difficult? Well, it was full of Koreans – which was understandable, given that it was bound for Seoul – but I couldn't understand a single word. The man sitting next to me spoke in an accent I struggled to grasp, especially when conversing with the air hostess, who understood him perfectly. And when they spoke in Korean, it felt exactly like watching Korean or Chinese dramas on Netflix, completely incomprehensible. I sorely missed subtitles.

After landing, I collected my single suitcase and headed towards the exit. A crowd of people stood with placards in their hands, most of them written in Korean characters. I grimaced, knowing I wouldn't understand any of them. But then, I spotted my name.

'Somasundaripriya Vibhuti Narayan' was boldly written on a placard held by a simple-looking man waiting for me.

Believe me when I say this, seeing my full name on display like that bothered me more than the thought of leaving my family behind to work in an entirely different country.

I stopped in front of the man and pointed at the placard, then at myself.

"You are Soma—" He paused to reread the placard, attempting to pronounce my name.

"I am Priya. You can call me Priya," I said quickly. In my embarrassment, it took me a moment to register that he could speak English fairly well, at least well enough for me to understand.

"Welcome to Seoul, madam," he said, bowing slightly before grabbing my suitcase. He glanced around, expecting to find more bags, but I had just the one. I also carried a laptop bag over my shoulder.

"It's just one," I smiled. He nodded, slightly puzzled, and led me outside. I didn't bother explaining that given my frequent travels I preferred to pack light.

"I will take you to the guesthouse," he informed me as he started the car.

"How far is the guesthouse from the office?" I asked.

"Ten minutes walking distance," he replied.

A ten-minute walk, I could manage that, I thought.

As I gazed out at the highway, my eyes landed on the stunning Seoul skyline. The view took my breath away. Hundreds of towering buildings surrounded a mountain nestled in the centre. Though the city was bathed in daylight now, I could only imagine how magical it would look at night when all the buildings were illuminated. On top of the mountain, I noticed what seemed like a large umbrella-like tower.

The tower looked amusing.

"What is that?" I asked, pointing at it.

"That is N Seoul Tower, one of the most famous landmarks in Seoul," the driver explained.

"Is it worth visiting?" I asked curiously.

"It definitely is," he nodded. "It offers a panoramic view of the city, it's beautiful."

My first instinct was to plan a visit. But then, another thought held me back. Who would I go with? Ever since I could remember, I had explored new places with Dhriti and our children. The idea of sightseeing without them filled me with guilt. How could I enjoy myself while they were stuck at home?

Their sad, sombre faces flashed before my eyes. None of them had told me not to go; they all knew how important this job was for us. But they were upset. I had promised daily video calls as a consolation and assured them I would be back in ten days.

"But then you'll leave again after just four days," our eldest, Rohan, had pointed out.

I had no response then, and I still had none. The only thing that had cheered them up was Dhriti's promise that I would bring back lots of chocolates and gifts.

"If you wish to go, you can call me. I'll take you there," my driver offered, bringing me back to the present. "That way, you won't be overcharged or struggle with the language."

His comment reminded me of something. "How are you speaking such clear English? I met a man on the flight, but his accent was so different that I couldn't understand a word," I said with a sigh.

"That's common here," he laughed. "Korean doesn't have certain sounds like 'F' and 'T.' 'F' often sounds like 'P,' and 'T' becomes more like 'Th'... so it can be confusing. But you'll get used to it."

"How do you speak such fluent English?" I asked, genuinely curious. He looked fully Korean.

"I'm half-Korean," he grinned. "My mother is Australian. She came here with her friends for a visit and never left."

"Why?" I asked, intrigued.

He chuckled. "She fell in love with my father. He was the group's delivery boy, and they fell for each other instantly, love at first sight, you know."

"Your father must be one handsome man," I teased.

"Oh, he is! I don't even compare," he laughed. And I had to admit, he was quite good-looking himself. Exceptionally fair, with symmetrical features and flawless skin.

"How did your mother cope with the language barrier?" I asked, hoping for some useful tips. "Honestly, no offense, but from what I've seen in videos, people in Korea don't always show emotions on their faces."

He burst into laughter. "No offense taken! It's true, my father rarely shows emotions."

"Then how did she manage? Your father probably didn't speak English back then, right?" I added.

"No, not a word," he admitted. "Even now, he struggles with English."

"Then how?" I pressed.

"My mom always says they understand each other through the language of love," he grinned.

"Language of love?" I repeated.

"That's what she calls it. Even though they've learned bits of each other's languages over the years, they still communicate without words. They even argue in their native tongues – Dad in Korean, Mom in English – and somehow, they always understand each other."

I let his words sink in. Maybe love doesn't need a language… it just needs two hearts willing to understand, even in silence. So, hopefully considering my situation, maybe, just maybe, language would not be the only way to communicate. Perhaps I, too, would find my own way to connect in this new place.

4

A sofa too low, a world too different

The driver, whose name I couldn't quite catch, dropped me off at the guest house and left. Before leaving, he handed me his calling card, saying I could call him whenever needed. Not wanting to take any chances, I saved his number in my phone immediately – just in case I lost the card later. It was a must-have for me.

I walked inside and found a girl sitting on a sofa.

"Soma---" she started with a smile.

"Priya," I corrected her instantly, extending my hand for a handshake. She shook it and gestured for me to sit beside her.

I lowered myself onto the seat, only to realize too late how low it actually was. I practically flopped down, my knees awkwardly jutting out. Meanwhile, she sat effortlessly, her legs tucked behind her knees, looking completely at ease.

"*Yoo weel get yoo-suh-tu eet, I am Ha-yoon,*" she said with a smile, her Korean-accented English more understandable this time.

"Hi Ha-yoon, yeah, I'm sure I'll get used to it," I replied, giving up on trying to sit like her and instead stretching my legs forward for comfort.

"*Hee-uh eez a mo-bile puh-one puh-yoo. Don' worry, eet eez een Eeng-lee-shuh, but yoo should yoo-suh eet so dat yoo don' pay-suh ee-shoo calling hee-uh. Boss-uh has assigned yoo a buh-dee, heez num-buh eez ahl-ready hee-uh, and hee weel be hee-uh short-lee. Break-pas' eez at se-ben in da morning, and dee-nuh eez at se-ben in da eeb-ning. Eef yoo ah not eat-eeng hee-uh, puh-lee-se in-puhm us buh-po hand, we don' wan' to way-suh puh-ood. Der eez a card een yoh room, puh-lee-se peel eet weet ahl dee-tails, een-cloo-deeng ah-nee puh-ood puh-puh-ren-suh and ah-luh-jees, and we weel take cay-uh of eet. And yoh room eez juss hee-uh. Room Too.*"

My jaw dropped as she delivered all of that in rapid English and handed me a key.

"I'm sorry, I didn't understand," I admitted, my voice softer than I intended.

She narrowed her eyes.

"*Yoo don' speek Eeng-lee-shuh?*" she asked, her tone almost accusing.

"I do speak and understand English—" I began, but before I could explain further, someone behind me launched into rapid Korean.

To me, it was pure gibberish.

I turned and saw an Indian-origin man standing there, smiling.

Ha-yoon handed me the key she had been holding and spoke quickly to the man. He nodded, responded in Korean, and she nodded back before leaving.

"Err…" I began once she was gone, but the boy interrupted me.

"Don't worry, I'll translate everything for you," he said with a reassuring smile.

"You speak English?" I exhaled in relief.

"I speak Hindi too. So if you ever miss your native language, we can talk in Hindi as well. I know I miss it," he grinned.

"I'm Priya," I introduced myself, struggling to stand up from the ridiculously low sofa before shaking his hand.

"I'm Chirag, and I'm your buddy here," he informed me.

"My buddy?" I echoed, perplexed.

"Ah yes, I am your buddy to help you around," he smiled.

"Okay, thanks," I laughed in relief. "What was Ha-yoon saying before?" I enquired. "It seemed important considering how offended she looked"

Chirag laughed, "Ha-yoon said that here is a mobile phone for you. Don't worry, it's in English, but you should use it so that you don't face network issues here," he explained, picking up a phone from the centre table and handing it to me. "Also, boss has assigned you a buddy, which is me, actually. My number is already in the phone, and I was supposed to arrive shortly, which I did," he grinned again. "Breakfast is at 7 in the morning, and dinner is at 7 in the evening. If you're not eating here, please inform the staff beforehand. They don't want to waste food. There's a card in your room, please fill it with all details, including any food preferences and allergies, and they'll take care of it. And your room is right here. Room 2," he pointed to the keys in my hands.

"Oh, so that's what she was saying," I laughed. "I couldn't understand a thing."

Chirag looked at me seriously, then sighed.

"What?" I asked.

"When I moved here five years ago, I had already been talking to the Korean team for months, so I at least understood their English. I learned Korean after moving here. It took me the better part of two years, but now I can speak it fluently. But you… you don't even understand their English. How will you survive?" he asked, shaking his head.

"I rarely spoke to our Korean counterparts back in Delhi, it was all on emails," I sighed as we walked to my room. "And honestly, until a few weeks ago, I had no idea I was coming here. So, well…"

"Well, better stay close to me then. I'll help you around," Chirag offered. "People here are generally good, and our colleagues are decent too. But they do get offended if someone doesn't understand their English. You saw Ha-yoon back there," he laughed, and I felt at ease with Chirag. He was easy going and felt like a nice man.

I unlocked my room, and my jaw dropped. Everything was so low… it was practically on the floor.

"You get used to it," Chirag said with a knowing sigh.

I placed my bag on the table and stared around. The room itself was clean and neat, but still, everything was at least a foot lower than what I was used to back home. How was my back supposed to survive this? Sitting for hours on the computer had already wrecked it, and something told me that living here would only make it worse.

"Or maybe you won't," Chirag grimaced. "I never did, so when I moved out of the guest house, I found an apartment with normal-height furniture. My home has a higher bed and regular seating."

Considering I couldn't exactly ask to move into his house, I sighed and sat on my bed, feeling absurdly out of place.

"How about I come back in two hours and take you to the office?" he suggested.

"I don't think I need two hours, but I'll call you," I said, pointing at my phone from India.

"Yes, and use that one," he gestured toward the new phone. "They gave you the latest model, which isn't even released yet. You can test it," he smiled and left.

Once I was alone, I studied the new phone, and only then did I really notice it. Yes, it was the latest model of ZenTel, one that cost a fortune. But, well… company paid, so...

I quickly checked the time. 10:45 AM in Seoul. My old phone showed 7:15 AM back home.

Everyone must be at home right now, and soon, the kids would be leaving for school. And I knew they must be worried about me.

So, without wasting another second, I saved Dhriti's number in my new phone and did a video call. And that's how I spent my first fifteen minutes in Seoul… with my family, hoping the next ten days would pass in a blur so I could be with them again.

5

Forks and first impressions

I was ready by noon and spent some time neatly putting away my clothes in the closet. By 12:15, I stepped out of my room and found Ha-yoon seated on the same sofa, her legs tucked comfortably beneath her once again.

She glanced at me and said something in rapid English. It was like words were dropping on my ears but I was unable to understand them. And I knew if she spoke slowly, I would understand!

I blinked at her, trying to process her words. She let out an impatient huff, grabbed a notepad, and scribbled something down. Then, shoving the paper into my hands rather briskly, she crossed her arms.

"The breakfast gets over at 9 each day, but just for today, you can have it now."

I read the note and smiled in understanding. "Please speak a little slowly," I asked feeling a bit scared.

She exhaled loudly and muttered something, though a little slowly. And hey, this time, I caught the meaning without trouble. She was, like everyone, wondering how I would possibly survive here.

"Thank you," I said, bowing slightly to show my appreciation. Thinking to myself that I was a survivor, that eventually I would figure this out, I followed the direction she was pointing.

As I entered the dining area, I spotted a man working behind a counter. Before I could say anything, Ha-yoon called out something in rapid Korean from behind me. The man listened, nodded, and then gestured for me to come closer as he picked up a bowl for my breakfast.

I texted Chirag after another twenty minutes, and he arrived in ten.

We walked out together, and I noticed a cycle standing outside. "It took me some time because I had to bring two cycles," he smiled, pointing at the second one meant for me.

"You travel here on cycles?" I asked, puzzled.

"Gee, girl, it seems you have not researched at all. Many people travel short distances on cycle here," he smiled.

"You travel by cycle too?" I asked, grabbing my own. It was a standard black bicycle, and I was glad he hadn't gone for some cliché pink one!

"Yes, I live a bit far away, and it takes me around twenty minutes on cycle. But I prefer this," he patted the seat of his cycle affectionately, "it helps keep me in shape," he smiled, now patting his stomach. He was very fit, indeed.

"How far are we from the office?" I asked, tucking in my stomach instinctively. I wasn't fat per se, but I wasn't particularly fit either.

"Ten minutes walking, less than five cycling," he grinned.

"Oh-kay!" I replied, positioning myself on the seat. "You know, I haven't cycled in more than two decades."

"Really?" he asked, shocked. He hopped off his cycle and stood beside me. "Try once. If you fall, I will catch you."

Feeling self-conscious, I tried. But after a shaky start, I managed to steady myself. Maybe it was true, you never really forget how to ride a bike!

"Amazing! Just turn left from here. I will catch up with you," he announced, and indeed, he did. Soon, we were both riding at a decent speed, the air rushing through my hair. And despite myself, I laughed, completely lost in the unexpected joy this brought.

We arrived in three minutes, and I couldn't believe that I had more fun in those three minutes than in the last three years. And just as quickly, guilt crept in at the thought.

"I like Seoul," I said as we parked our cycles and locked them. "It's so peaceful. Back home, it's so loud, and people are very nosy."

"Seoul is like that too. We're actually not in the heart of the city, we're much closer to the outskirts. That's why it feels peaceful. But the main city? It's just like Delhi, believe me. Although I'd agree, Seoul is much less polluted and there's less honking," he said, rolling his eyes dramatically, as if recalling how people in India constantly blare their horns at traffic signals, "but crowded and loud for sure," he finished.

I nodded as we entered the building. He led me to the reception to get my ID badge.

"Your badge will get you access to most floors, but not the top floor, that's for top tiers only. And you won't be allowed in the server rooms either; only IT folks have access there, okay?" he informed me. I nodded.

We walked to the elevator, and he pressed the number 2.

"And people are very nosy here too," he added as we stepped out. "Believe me when I say this, it's actually lucky that Ha-yoon cannot speak to you. She's a blabbermouth. Anything you say to her, or even don't say, will spread everywhere."

"I see," I sighed, already feeling irked.

"This is my seat. Why don't you sit here?" He pointed to the empty spot next to him. "It's vacant, so you can use it. And do you know the best part…" he grinned… "all desks are adjustable along with chairs, so, wherever you sit, just adjust the height to Indian style and you will be comfortable."

Feeling relieved, I nodded. Just then, a girl walked over and started speaking to him in Korean, completely ignoring me. I took that as my cue to pull out my laptop and start setting up.

"Oh no, not this one," Chirag interrupted as he saw my laptop. "That won't work here. I got yours ready," and he handed me a brand-new laptop.

The girl next to him said something in Korean, her expression mildly irritated, but Chirag casually responded before helping me turn on the laptop, he already knew the password and security key.

"How about we grab some lunch before we start working?" he suggested as I checked my emails. There were a few waiting for me.

I wasn't particularly hungry, but I agreed just to be polite.

"Is the European coder here as well?" I asked as we walked.

"Yes, he arrived last night. I met him briefly this morning, but since I had to fetch you, I didn't get a chance to talk much."

As we neared the cafeteria, I turned to him. "So, that girl who was talking to you…" I started. "Is she your girlfriend?"

"Who? Ahn Shi?" Chirag did a double take at my question.

"If that's her name," I smiled.

"No, no! Shi and I are just friends. My parents would disown me if I married anyone other than an Indian girl," he laughed. "They want me to marry a Gujarati girl, but given my current relationship status, they'd settle for someone from another state too. But Korean? Oh, big NO!"

I chuckled, shaking my head. Parental expectations were truly universal.

"Why do you ask if she was my girlfriend?" Chirag asked curiously.

"She didn't like me much," I muttered.

"Ah, Shi doesn't like many people, just ignore her," he said, brushing his hands carelessly, as if it were a daily occurrence. But I knew he was wrong. That Shi had feelings for him, and even though he didn't reciprocate, it could come back to bite me if she got the wrong idea!

"Do you want to eat at the table or on the floor?" he asked as we entered the cafeteria. There were two sections: one with tables, though their height was far from regular for me, unfortunately! And then there was a section where everyone sat on the floor, barefoot.

I was debating where we should sit when I spotted a man who was clearly not Korean and was walking towards the sitting section.

"Alex," Chirag called out, and the man stopped.

He had a tray laden with food and smiled when he saw Chirag before making a beeline for us. Chirag led me toward the food section.

"Hello," Alex greeted us with a warm smile.

"This is Priya," Chirag introduced.

"Oh, you're Alex Lorenzo, from Germany," I said, suddenly remembering.

"Yes, the one and only. And you are…?" he paused, clearly having already forgotten my name.

Weird. I had interacted with him multiple times over calls. Was he really that forgetful, or was he just being rude?

"I'm Priya. I was called here to work on the new tech," I replied.

"Same. But I was under the impression that Somasundaripriya was coming, not someone else. You know, I came only to work with Somasundaripriya," Alex said, emphasizing my full name. His expression shifted from polite curiosity to clear disappointment.

"I am her," I pointed to myself. "Though I go by Priya, not that. Which, I must say, I'm quite surprised, your pronunciation of my full name is flawless," I added with a laugh.

"You are Somasundaripriya?" Alex asked, setting his tray down on the next table and grabbing both my hands, shaking them enthusiastically.

He was in his fifties, well-experienced, and reputedly very helpful. He apologized for not recognizing me earlier, but I waved it off.

"I have been dying to meet you! I could kiss you right now." And judging by his expression, he might actually do it!

"I think you should refrain from kissing anyone, Alex," Chirag chortled. "They are very strict about professional etiquette here."

"Oh, you know what I mean," Alex laughed again, still clasping my hands. "Your firewall code was exquisite and remarkable! When I heard that its coder was no more than twenty-five at the time, I became a huge fan, massive fan!"

Chirag subtly extricated my hands from Alex's grasp, and we filled our trays with food. I took only a little since I wasn't very hungry.

"Somasundaripriya, where do you want to sit?" Alex asked, and I was once again amazed at how easily he pronounced my full name. I, however, grimaced.

"Please call me Priya. Just Priya," I insisted.

"Okay. I was asked to sit there," he said, pointing to the section where everyone sat on the floor, with one empty table standing out.

"Let's sit there then," I said, noticing that despite that table being empty, no one was approaching it. This one table was placed far from others, just next to the kitchen door. But I didn't think its location was an issue. I felt something else was alienating it. Because it was excluded thoroughly, like no one was even considering it when looking for seats, as if it was not even there.

However, despite my thoughts, Alex and I sat down, but Chirag remained standing, his face twisting with unease.

"What's wrong?" I asked, noting his discomfort.

"Is this where you were asked to sit? On this very table?" Chira g questioned Alex in a low voice, staring around.

"Yes, they specifically asked me to sit here," Alex nodded.

"Are you sure? And who is 'they', because this is..." Chirag trailed off as a man appeared in front of us. Carrying a tray of food, he placed it down right in front of me and sat.

I stared at the man, he was singularly interested in his plate and was not at all bothered to take note that he had just joined three people at lunch.

Alex was still talking to me, "You really don't like your full name?" But before I could answer, Chirag spoke.

"Mr Choi," he bowed as he addressed the man. "I'm sorry, we didn't…"

Mr Choi responded in rapid Korean, and Chirag visibly tensed before abruptly sitting beside me. His stunned expression didn't go unnoticed.

I turned to Chirag, whispering, "*Kya hua*?" (translation: what happened?)

But he didn't answer and just shook his head.

Mr Choi, however, seemed to understand my question. He looked up and tilted his head slightly in my direction, but his expression remained unreadable. I had the distinct feeling he was sizing me up.

His features were striking, sharp yet perfectly symmetrical. His amber-coloured eyes, his tousled dark hair, and his porcelain-like skin gave him an almost unreal appearance. His lips, oh God! his lips were so unnaturally red, as if they had been painted, yet their slight indentations proved otherwise.

Unconsciously, I licked my own lips and felt their roughness.

He cocked a brow, clearly aware that I had been staring... staring at his lips! And I just knew he was silently asking me 'do you like what you see?'

Feeling awkward, I lowered my gaze to my tray. It had some rice and noodles. I picked up my spoon and took a bite of rice. It wasn't particularly to my taste, but I had little choice.

As I ate, I looked around and noticed that now everyone was staring at us… were we not supposed to sit here? However, what else struck me as odd was that girls, almost all the girls, were staring at Mr Choi. Some were even stopping pointedly right in front of him so that he noticed them.

I was very confused! I mean he was handsome yes, but were these girls crazy? I looked around more and it confused me even more. I had a distinct feeling that more than six girls wanted to come and sit in my place but were resisting the urge.

As my eyes fell back on my food, I realized Mr Choi was looking at me intrigued.

"*Khana khao!*" Chirag hissed under his breath. (translation: eat your food)

But I was too stunned to eat. Was this normal Korean behaviour? Literally drooling over one guy!

"*Ye sab ladkiya pagal hain kya?*" I muttered to Chirag. (translation: all these girls are crazy or what?)

And Mr Choi's head tilted further towards us, a small smirk playing on his lips as if he understood what I meant. Could he understand Hindi?

"Later," Chirag whispered and jabbed his spoon towards my plate. "Eat!" he insisted.

He was epically stressed, so, I just shook my head and started to eat.

"Try the noodles, they're good," Alex pointed at my tray.

I nodded and glanced around, this time focussing on people's trays and yes, everyone else was eating noodles. Picking up the metal chopsticks, I attempted to hold them like the others.

"Try it like this," Chirag said, adjusting my grip, guiding my fingers. But no matter how hard I tried, I couldn't get the hang of it.

Chirag even took my hand, attempting to manoeuvre it properly, but it was hopeless.

"Or I could feed you the noodles," Chirag offered lightly.

"I don't think so," I muttered, cursing myself for not bringing the fork I had taken from the airplane. At this moment, I wished I were back in my room, eating comfortably at a proper table.

"I guess you people don't have forks here," I whispered to Chirag.

He shook his head. "I struggled a lot initially too, but I learned eventually."

Mr Choi, who had been silently watching me all this time, suddenly raised his hand in the air.

A man appeared instantly. Mr Choi spoke to him in rapid Korean. The man looked visibly shocked but bowed and left after another firm command from Mr Choi.

"What was that about?" I whispered to Chirag.

He just shrugged.

I turned back to Mr Choi. He was still looking at me.

Feeling flustered, I quickly glanced at Alex and Chirag, they were focused on their food, oblivious to whatever was happening between Mr Choi and me.

The man who had taken Mr Choi's order returned, speaking in Korean before handing something to me wrapped in a tissue paper.

"He said he found only one, so please don't throw it away," Chirag translated.

I unwrapped the object, and Chirag's jaw practically hit the floor.

A fork.

As far as I knew, forks weren't used in South Korea. Yet, here it was, in my hands.

I looked at Mr Choi. His face remained expressionless as he stared at his food. But when his gaze flickered up to meet mine, I saw it, he had done this for me. Why?!

Chirag muttered something under his breath, but I didn't care. Elation bloomed inside me as I dug my fork into the noodles and took a satisfied bite.

And as the smile spread across my face, it was mirrored, just barely, on Mr Choi's lips.

And in that moment I knew that between Chirag, Alex, and now Mr Choi, maybe, just maybe, my time here wouldn't be so unbearable after all. Because in their presence, especially *his*, this new place would feel less strange, less scary… and the loneliness it carried wouldn't hurt quite as much.

6

A meeting in the dark

After lunch, Chirag led me back to my desk. Alex, as it turned out, sat just two rows down from me. Before long, he appeared beside me, eager to discuss what was expected of us here. But as it turned out, neither of us had a clue. So, side by side, we dove into our tasks, figuring things out as we went.

Chirag was so busy that I never got the chance to ask him about Mr Choi. I made a mental note to corner him later.

By the time the clock struck four, an email popped into both Alex's and my inbox, summoning us to the fifth floor. Alex and I walked together, still chatting. He was easy-going, light-hearted, and, frankly, good company. Married with four kids back in Germany, he had an effortless way of making conversation. And, not to mention, he was incredibly flattering. He kept asking me about my codes and latest developments, and I found myself answering simply, yet with a growing sense of pride.

The fifth floor was unexpectedly dark. I mean, really dark… so much so that I wondered if the electricity had gone out. A few computer screens glowed eerily, casting dim silhouettes of people working. The rhythmic clicking of keyboards was the only sound in the otherwise silent space.

"Why is it so dark in here?" I whispered, my voice carrying unnervingly in the hush. For a moment, the typing stopped. Then, just as suddenly, it resumed.

"Umm..." Alex began but then fell silent again.

A door creaked open on the other side of the floor, and a flood of light spilled out. There, bathed in the glow, stood Mr Choi, waiting. The sudden illumination revealed a small workspace: two people, one woman and one man, sat at their stations, each surrounded by four screens. The eerie darkness now confined to a manageable space, Alex and I hurried toward the room, grateful we wouldn't have to fumble our way through.

Inside, Alex bowed deeply. I followed suit, bowing too.

It was a small meeting room with four chairs and thick walls. I guessed the room had no windows, to maintain the darkness outside, which, to be honest, felt oddly creepy.

Mr Choi spoke in Korean, and Alex responded in kind. I sat frozen. How was I supposed to participate if they spoke only in Korean?

"I…" Mr Choi started, "don't… a… speak English… a… well…" His words were slow, deliberate, and tinged with an accent, yet perfectly understandable. Though his added *a* may be a problem!

"I can translate. I know more than six languages," Alex said proudly.

I smiled at him but felt a twinge of frustration. Even with Alex translating, I would still be on the sidelines of the conversation.

"I… a… find… way you not… a… left out," Mr Choi spoke thoughtfully. "Give… a… time to… a… me."

I understood him, and I also understood he was adding *a*… to think his next word in english. But I blinked in surprise. He understood what I was thinking. That realization sent a ripple of curiosity through me.

"I'm sorry, but... who exactly are you?" I asked, bluntly.

Alex whipped his head toward me, looking as if I had just slapped him.

Mr Choi, however, only smiled, amused. Before he could answer, Alex jumped in, "He is Mr Choi Mirae-Jun, the head programmer of ZenTel and—"

Mr Choi simply raised a hand, silencing Alex effortlessly.

Oh. So this was the man, the mastermind behind ZenTel's inventions and innovations. Damn it! I should have known about him.

"Sorry, I always thought…" I trailed of. "You design all these phones and cutting-edge gadgets?" I asked, suddenly feeling very, very small in his presence.

"I help," Mr Choi replied with a smile.

"Oh, he's so modest. And so young!" Alex chortled. "I can't believe I'm the oldest in this group."

I could see why Alex was surprised. Because that's what I always thought too. I always imagined Choi Mirae-Jun to be an old man, much *much* more experienced than this… than this…

"How old are you?" I blurted out, then immediately regretted it.

Mr Choi's brow lifted slightly, but then he smiled. "Twenty-nine," he replied.

What? To be the brain behind everything ZenTel produced, he had to be a genius, and he was only twenty-nine!

"Wow!" That was the only word I could utter.

"Anyway," Mr Choi continued, "wait," he raised his hand and quickly spoke something into his tablet, then read aloud, "I am emailing you both my latest code. Please have a look, and we will regroup tomorrow."

And with that, the man dismissed us.

I turned to leave when he spoke again. "Soma—" he hesitated, attempting my name.

"Priya. It's just Priya, Mr Choi," I smiled.

"Priya," he repeated, returning the smile. Then, with a flick of his hand, he motioned for Alex to leave.

Alex gave us both a fleeting look before stepping out.

Once alone, Mr Choi began speaking quickly into his tablet, then read aloud: "Thank you for being here. I know you didn't want to, but I had to bring you here to finalize our tech."

I nodded grimly.

He spoke in Korean again, then read from his tablet, "Your boss fought tooth and nail to keep you there." My head snapped up. Ashok never mentioned fighting for me to stay!

"He wanted to come here himself," Mr Choi added.

My eyebrows shot up, though deep down I was not surprised! "But Ashok doesn't know coding," I stated plainly.

Mr Choi spoke once more in his tablet and then read the translation: "That's why I had to have you. What use do I have for him here? He drove a hard bargain, but I allowed everything. I think having you for even a month will be far more valuable than having him here for a year."

I smiled at the compliment and bowed slightly.

"Thank you, Mr Choi. It means a lot coming from someone like you. You're a genius," I replied genuinely. But he had an amused expression on his face, so I continued, "I am not flattering or anything. I mean, you *are* a genius. How else would you be the head programmer of a billion-dollar corporation, Mr Choi?"

"Call me CJ," he suggested. "Or even better, call me Mirae. My friends call me Mirae."

I froze.

"Mirae?" I echoed, stunned. "You go by Mirae?"

"Mirae, my name, yes," he nodded, looking slightly puzzled.

"It's a pleasure to meet you, CJ," I said, shaking his hand. I wasn't quite ready to call him Mirae. Because though he would never know, his name was special to me… because some names don't just introduce a person… they stay with you, quietly, long after the moment has passed. "You have no idea how much I love your name."

He looked confused, but I simply smiled and stepped out into the darkened floor.

7

Only if Google could translate!

As I walked back to my desk, I felt the weight of every gaze following me. Confused by the sudden attention, I reached my desk and looked at Chirag, who wore an intrigued expression.

"What?" I asked, feeling awkward.

"Did you really ask Mr Choi who he was? And how old he is?" he demanded.

"I mean, now I know he's the head programmer, why is that such a big deal?" I said as I entered my password and fired up my laptop.

"He is…" Chirag started, but before he could finish, I swore loudly, turning more than a few heads in my direction.

Chirag looked positively scandalized by my choice of words.

"Sorry, but this is all in Korean!" I muttered, lowering my voice, as I pointed at my screen.

"What is in Korean?" he asked, shifting his seat closer.

"This," I pointed again at my screen. The code CJ had sent me was entirely in Korean, which meant it was nothing but a jumble of strange symbols to me. I couldn't make sense of a single word.

"You are in Korea now, Priya," Chirag stated the obvious.

"I know but still… How am I supposed to study this overnight and discuss with him tomorrow?" I demanded.

"You can't study it overnight because you're not allowed to take that laptop out of the office premises," Chirag informed me.

"What?" I blinked at him in shock.

"If they were comfortable letting you take this code out of the office's secure network, I'm sure they would have just emailed it to you back in India," Chirag explained.

"Fair point," I admitted. "So, how am I supposed to…" I trailed off as my eyes landed on Alex. He was calmly studying the code at his desk, completely unfazed.

"Alex," I called out, walking over to him.

He barely glanced up before demanding, "What did Mr Choi want with you without me?" His tone was sharp, his expression a little too guarded. Was he… jealous?!

"Err… he was just telling me how my boss back in India wanted to come here instead of me, but Mr Choi didn't want him, he wanted me because I can actually code, and my boss can't," I said, keeping my answer simple.

At my words, Alex visibly relaxed.

"Of course. Your boss is nothing compared to you," he beamed.

I let out a small laugh. "Anyway, the code is in Korean," I pointed out.

"Yes, I can read Korean," he said, smiling smugly.

Of course, he could. I resisted the urge to groan. I was the only fool who had come all the way to a foreign country without knowing the language or even understanding the damn accent.

"How about I help you?" he suggested. "It's actually not that big. I can go through the entire code in a few hours and then give you a complete breakdown. What do you think?"

"Thanks," I said, though something told me that relying entirely on Alex wasn't the wisest option. I needed a backup plan.

So, I turned to the next best thing.

Google Translate.

Scrolling to the end of the code, I saw it had 2,197 lines. And I knew I could not feed in the code into Google. I would have to feed the symbols one at a time, which would be a very, no, incredibly difficult task. So, pushing up my sleeves, I braced myself because it was going to be a long night.

By 7:20 PM, I had managed to translate 511 lines when my phone chimed. The number was unknown, but I answered anyway.

"Hello?" I said, rubbing my eyes.

"This is Ha-yoon speaking," came the slow, deliberately clear voice on the other end. Strange how she couldn't talk like this in person.

"Hi, Ha-yoon," I replied, instinctively glancing at the clock on my laptop.

"Dinner time," she snapped.

I groaned.

"Yes, I'll be there soon," I sighed, but before I could say anything else, she hung up.

Jumping to my feet, I turned to Chirag.

"I have two questions," I announced.

"Fire away," he replied, eyes still glued to his screen.

"Where do I keep this laptop while I'm away? And can I come back later in the evening, after dinner, to continue working?"

That got his attention. Chirag looked at me, bemused.

"Why do you want to come back?" he asked.

"Because I'm only on line 511, and I have more than 2,000 lines to decode and understand before tomorrow morning," I explained.

Chirag gave me an incredulous look before shaking his head with a smile.

"Fine. But no one works past 8 here, Priya. You'll be completely alone," he warned.

"That's fine. It's not like I have anything better to do back at the guest house," I muttered. "So, where do I leave the laptop?"

"Here," he tossed me a small key. "Lock it before you go."

I did as instructed, and secured the laptop in my desk drawer before heading out.

As I was stepping out, Chirag joined me, "Would you like to have dinner with me tonight?"

I smiled. "Maybe some other day. Ha-yoon just called, and honestly… that woman scares me."

"Yeah, she scares me too," he admitted with a chuckle. "I'll join you then. After dinner, we can head back together."

I nodded, and we left.

The streets were eerily quiet.

"Is it safe at night here?" I asked, watching the deserted roads as we rode to the guesthouse.

"It's safer than Delhi, but I'd still be cautious," Chirag warned. "I'll ride with you back to the office, but when you leave, make sure to have a security guard with you, okay?"

I agreed, of course, safety first!

8

An answer, but a million questions

At the guest house, Ha-yoon didn't look thrilled that Chirag was joining me for dinner, but thankfully, she didn't stop him either.

Post dinner, I had a quick video call with my family, changed into more comfortable clothes, and then we rode back to the office.

Alone in the empty space, I sat at my desk, translating one line after another as the hours ticked by.

Tap! Tap! Tap!

I jerked awake, blinking rapidly as I looked around in confusion.

"What?" I mumbled, rubbing my face groggily.

"What doing here?" CJ asked, his tone serious. He stood just outside my cubicle, arms crossed, staring at me like I had lost my mind.

"I was working last night," I mumbled, hastily wiping the drool off my face.

"Morning now," he pointed out. I followed his gaze out the window, and sure enough, the office was already bathed in the morning glow.

"Oh no! I must have dozed off around three, I guess," I groaned, stretching. "And I'm still 200 lines short."

At my words, CJ's face morphed into something dangerously close to concern.

"You working till three? What is short?" he demanded, stepping into my space to glance at my laptop screen. He was so close that the scent of his perfume overpowered my sleepy clogs.

"I was translating," I yawned, hastily covering my mouth with my hand, ugh, morning breath.

CJ ran a hand through his hair, groaning as if I had personally offended him. "Why… a… not tell this?" he pointed at my screen in exasperation.

"I was going to write a script to auto-translate it into English. I think I've gathered enough data to train my model to do it," I explained quickly, still speaking through my hand.

"I…" he started, but then stopped himself. With a resigned sigh, he pulled out his tablet, did the same routine as yesterday, spoke something in Korean, and then read the translated text aloud.

"I already have a model that translates codes into all languages where our offices are situated," he read from his tablet.

My hand dropped from my face.

"All you needed to do was ask!" he added, reading from his tablet with a slight shake of his head.

A thousand – no, a million – curses swirled in my mind at that moment, but I bit my tongue. It wasn't his fault. These things happened.

"Never mind that now," I huffed, hastily shutting my laptop and locking it away in my desk. "I'm going to freshen up."

As I started to walk away, he suddenly said something in quick Korean. I turned, confused, watching him as he repeated himself in Korean but with a few gestures. Instinctively, I replied,

"I'll come find you when I'm back, yeah."

CJ froze. His expression was priceless… he looked stunned and even a little impressed. Did I really understand him? Or was he just shocked by how naturally I had answered?

"Wait… what did you say just now?" I asked, just as confused as he looked. "I'm too sleepy. I think I just spoke randomly."

He quickly spoke into his tablet and read out the translation.

"I did say, 'Come find me once you have rested.'"

My eyebrows shot up.

"I'll be back in about two hours," I told him, watching him as he nodded, still looking slightly perplexed.

"How… a… you… a… under---stand?" he asked, his English even more broken than usual.

I laughed lightly. "I don't know, I just did!" But as I walked away, a new thought struck me: I had no idea how I understood him, but how in hell did he understand everything I said in English or even Hindi for that matter. He barely knew more than a handful of words. And his English was worse than the helper we had in office back in Delhi! Weird, huh!

It was still early, just 6 AM, so I quickly rode back to the guesthouse, showered, and got dressed just in time for breakfast.

As I sat down with my plate, Ha-yoon sidled up next to me, her usual scrutinizing expression in place.

"Ah… I notice you not come back last night? Everything… alright?" she asked carefully, her words slow and deliberate.

I looked up at her, mid-sip of my tea. "Hey! I can understand you better now," I smiled, realizing it only now.

She waved a hand airily, "You get used to it." Then, leaning in slightly, she asked, "So, where were you last night?"

"Office. Was working." I shrugged, taking a bite of my toast.

"Ah! Was that Chiraaag boy with you too?" she asked, her tone just a little too curious. Her smile a little too knowing!

I stopped mid-bite and looked at her, absolutely stunned. I hated nosy people!

"No, he dropped me at the office and went home. Why?" I asked simply.

"Nothing," she grinned innocently, but I wasn't buying it.

"Oh, you should not work so hard. It is just your first day. Take it slow," she added, all fake concern and empty smiles.

Something about her didn't sit right with me, and Chirag's words echoed in my head: *She's dangerous.*

I set my fork down and gave her a polite but firm smile. "I'm here to work, so I'm working. And on that note, I'm late." I downed the rest of my tea, grabbed my bag and my precious fork, and got up.

Thanks to time difference, it was still too early to call home, so I sent Dhriti a quick text to call me when they all woke up and headed out.

Maybe Chirag was right. There was something about Ha-yoon that I couldn't put my finger on, but it definitely wasn't good. I had no idea where she passed on all the information she collected, but then again, why should I care? It wasn't like I had anything to hide.

The first thing I did upon reaching the office was drop an IM on the office network to CJ. I had noticed his name before, tagged in emails back in India, but I never imagined I would actually meet him. He was a big hotshot, and everyone, and I mean, everyone was terrified of him. But I didn't find him scary. Instead, I found him… welcoming, comforting, even.

"I am back," I texted CJ.

"So soon?" he replied almost instantly.

Okay, another surprise! CJ was infamous for not replying to messages. Apparently, he was always far too busy. But he replied to me… and that too instantly.

"Yes, I am here. Let me know if you need me to do anything," I responded formally.

With that, I turned my focus back to finishing the code translation. Sure, he had said he already had a translated version, but I wanted to do it myself too. There was something satisfying about doing things my own way. Once I was done, I started working on an agent that would translate everything from Korean to English. I was slowly getting accustomed to the English accent here, but understanding Korean? That was a whole different battle.

I was still working when someone tapped on my desk. I looked up, blinking in surprise.

There he was. Smiling at me.

"Break-fasht?" CJ said simply.

I hesitated. I had already eaten, but... still, I nodded.

I reached out to lock my laptop in my desk, but he simply pointed at my bag, laptop, and other things.

"Bring, come..." And he started to walk.

Every head was turned at me... what the hell was wrong with people.

Chirag, who had just fired up his own laptop, looked thoroughly confused.

"Coming?" I asked Chirag, and without a second thought, he joined me. However, as we walked, just a few steps behind CJ, a girl stumbled and fell, right in CJ's arms.

"Are you okay?" I hurried forward and asked the girl as CJ steadied her.

The girl said something in Korean, not to me but to CJ, and left.

CJ huffed, he looked mildly irritated, and Chirag smirked. Chirag had not even moved to help the girl, and I had an inkling that in this situation it was not the girl who needed help, but CJ!

We sat at the same table as yesterday, the only empty one in the entire cafeteria. Again, it struck me as odd. Even though some people were still standing, looking for seats, no one occupied this table.

I leaned toward Chirag and whispered, "Is this table reserved for him?"

"Yes, after all, he is..." he started but then stopped.

I followed his gaze to CJ. For a second, I could've sworn I saw CJ shake his head.

"What are you not telling me?" I demanded, looking back at Chirag.

But he just shook his head.

I was about to push further, but CJ said something in Korean. Chirag's reaction was immediate, his head bowed slightly, and he nodded.

A flicker of irritation flared inside me.

"You know it is rude to do this, CJ," I snapped, maybe a little too loudly from Korean standards.

A sharp intake of breath rippled through the cafeteria. Several people gasped, their eyes darting toward us.

I ignored them.

"You can't just order him around in Korean," I continued, but in much lower voice. "He is my friend and you cannot stop him from telling me things. He has every right to say whatever he wishes."

Only then did I realize how much I had leaned toward Chirag. Too close. Too familiar.

CJ, who had been about to speak, stilled. His eyes flickered to the space – no, the lack of space – between me and Chirag.

He said nothing.

"Seedhe baitho, mujhe marwaoge kya?" Chirag hissed under his breath. (Translation: Sit straight. Do you want me dead or what?)

CJ's head snapped in our direction. His expression unreadable.

Wait! Did he just understand that too?

"You can understand Hindi too!" I observed, "can't you?"

CJ didn't reply, instead, he just glared at us… more so at Chirag. I was about to say something, but my phone rang, a video call from home. Perfect timing. I excused myself and stepped onto the open veranda, the cool breeze a welcome relief.

Twenty minutes later, I returned.

The cafeteria was almost empty, only a few stragglers and CJ remained now. He was sitting with his laptop open, his plate already empty. Why was he still here? Was he waiting for me? I wanted to ask him so many things, but instead, I asked, "Chirag left?" I settled into my seat and picked up my spoon to eat what was now a very cold breakfast.

CJ nodded, though he looked irritated and I somehow knew it was because I had asked about Chirag.

I glanced at him. Then, without thinking, I blurted, "Why do you treat Chirag like he's *your* employee?"

His eyes narrowed slightly.

"He's a nice man, CJ. You shouldn't be rude to him."

A muscle in his jaw twitched. I knew I had just gotten here, and I had no right to speak to him that way, but I wasn't the one who let others do whatever they pleased!

"You like him?" he asked abruptly.

I blinked.

"I got here only yesterday," I stated the obvious.

"So, that's a yes?" he challenged.

I felt rattled, so I replied instantly, "Of course, it is a yes. He's my buddy here. My friend," I nodded. "Why shouldn't I like him?"

CJ studied me for a moment. Then, instead of answering, he said something else.

"But he *likes* you."

I paused.

Then, I frowned.

"Like I said, he's my buddy, my friend. Why shouldn't he like me too?"

CJ gave me a long look, like I was the biggest fool he had ever met. I shifted in my seat, suddenly feeling warm. Why was he looking at me like that?

But instead of replying, he just said, "Whatever!" or something similar in Korean. He gestured, and a man appeared almost instantly to clean his plate.

The way people behaved around him… a sudden realization began to dawn upon me. What if he was more than just an employee, what if… But just then, a convoy of people entered the cafeteria.

Everyone jumped to their feet, and I realized it was *the* Mr Choi. The owner of ZenTel.

He stopped in front of CJ, just beside me, and started shouting in Korean. CJ listened with his head bowed, and after a while, he stood up, still with his head low. Mr Choi, the owner, looked at me sharply; I, too, jumped to my feet and moved around the table to get some distance from this horrid man. I could not understand a word he saying but it was clear he was very mean and rude!

Mr Choi went on berating CJ. Twice I wanted to say something, but each time I even thought of speaking, I felt CJ twitch, as if warning me not to. So, I stayed quiet.

After what felt like hours, Mr Choi finally left. I looked around, everyone else had vanished too. The cafeteria was empty. Even the kitchen staff was gone. Only CJ and I remained.

I wanted to ask what that had all been about, but I was just too incensed to even form words. No matter what the situation was, no one had the right to speak to someone like that, especially not in front of everyone!

"What the f-ck was that?" I swore as CJ sat down again.

"That was Mr Choi," CJ huffed. "No swearing," he chided, attempting a small smile.

"How can he treat you like that?" I demanded dropping beside him. Just before he had walked into the cafeteria, I was almost certain CJ was the owner of ZenTel, after all he was treated with such intense reverence. But now... but now it seemed like CJ was in an even worse position than I was!

"He owns us all," CJ spoke slowly, carefully putting his words together. "He can do as he likes."

"Screw that," I exclaimed indignantly. "No one has a right to speak like this... not to you, or anyone else."

CJ grabbed my hand and looked into my eyes as he spoke in a barely audible whisper, "Not use that... a... language here..." His tone was soft, urgent. He whispered something more in Korean, but I didn't quite catch it. Because my entire body had frozen at his touch. He was still holding my hand, and it was sending shivers up and down my spine.

CJ seemed to realize what he was doing. He pulled away quickly and sat back.

To shake off the moment, I grabbed my laptop and spoke in a rush.

"For the record, next time I am going to bite his head off if he is rude to you again," I growled because I had to get that off my chest, CJ looked at me amused, "And I know you have a translating agent, but I had nothing to do, so I wrote one too."

I passed him my laptop, eager – desperate, really – to change the subject.

As he scanned through my work, his eyes brightened. He didn't say a word, but I could tell he was impressed.

I finished eating, and then he led me out. But instead of heading back to my desk, we went somewhere else entirely.

The dark floor.

Only… it wasn't dark at all. In fact, it was brightly lit, and now, completely empty.

"My cabin," he said, pointing.

I followed his gesture to a large glass-walled office. Inside, there was nothing but computer screens. So many screens.

"Your seat," he added, pointing to a desk right outside.

I frowned. "But wasn't someone else sitting here?"

I distinctly remembered four screens. Two people.

"They move. You, Alex sit here with me, so we work together."

I hesitated. Something about the way he said it made my stomach flip.

But before I could think too hard, he pulled out the chair for me.

Feeling weird, yet oddly smitten, I sat down.

"How many screens you need?" he asked, gesturing toward the array of monitors surrounding the room.

"Two," I replied. Which, conveniently, were already set up for me.

He nodded once, then disappeared into his own cabin.

From my seat, I could see him.

And he… could see me.

I tried to focus on finishing my agent. But I kept getting distracted.

Thirty minutes later, Alex arrived and took his seat.

And finally the work resumed.

9

If I could, I would love you

Four days passed in a haze of discussions and developments. I had never worked on such complex algorithms before, and getting onboarded was no easy feat. Alex was new to this too, but CJ was an expert. He guided us through every nuance with precision, and thanks to his help, along with hours of online reading, by Friday evening, I was finally starting to get a hang of it.

But what I wasn't getting a hang of was my schedule and a few other things. Speaking of schedule, though I had managed to avoid pulling all-nighters, I was still the first one to arrive and almost always the last to leave, which left me tired to the bone. Alex usually left around 8 in the evening, and while I stepped out at 7 PM for dinner, I always returned and worked until just past midnight, leaving with a security guard, of course. CJ, however, always disappeared around 5 PM and never came back until the next morning. Alex and I often wondered where he went, but neither of us ever voiced it aloud.

And about other things, well… only I called him CJ. Alex, Chirag and everyone else I came in contact with in the four days called him Mr Choi. Feeling weird, when I addressed him as Mr Choi, he gave me a sharp look, making me change back to CJ automatically. And not to mention our chats. Though he mainly spoke Korean or broken English, in the past four days, I understood him perfectly well… and I kind of fought with him, a lot! Or should I say disagreed with him almost twenty times, while Alex always nodded and accepted whatever he said.

"You are either way too stupid or way too brave," Alex had commented when CJ had stormed in his cabin after a rather hot argument with me, to which Alex had not participated at all!

"What? I don't just bend over backward for anyone!" I snapped, feeling irritated.

Alex raised his eyebrows at my comment, because truth be told, he was bending over backwards for CJ, following his every word.

"You know what I mean," I hissed, "If I have an idea or a different opinion, I am going to voice it. I don't think he brought us here just to follow his orders," I spoke pointing towards his office, just realizing that he was staring at me.

Was he furious with me? I couldn't say!

One other thing that happened in the past week was that I took on a silent mission, i.e., saving CJ from way-too-opportune girls. When I saw yet another girl stumble and fall into his arms, I decided enough was enough. From then on,

I made it a point to walk beside him every day to and from the cafeteria.

Which also meant that I sometimes had to drag CJ for the lunch hour! He was a workaholic, and if he was working on something, he would just shush us away and not eat. But I, well, I know what empty stomach does to mind, so I dragged him along always… and though he didn't let anyone do it to him, my incessant whining about how hungry I was, while standing at his door, always did the trick.

So yeah, now I walked beside him and, somehow, I had developed a sixth sense for spotting girls aiming for a 'chance' encounter. So whenever I saw one inching closer, I'd casually reposition myself to make sure she always ended up on my side instead of his. It might have looked normal from the outside, but honestly? It was exhausting… switching sides every so often, especially considering cafeteria was quite far away from fifth floor!

CJ found it amusing. Chirag and Alex found it absolutely hilarious.

"What?" I asked Chirag on Thursday as CJ went to use the washroom.

"I have never seen Mr Choi this regular in the cafeteria before, these girls are getting frantic," Chirag murmured as he looked around. And yes, more and more girls were crowding cafeteria off late.

"If she won't bully him into coming, he won't eat," Alex chuckled.

"I don't bully him," I spoke, alarmed.

"No, you just stand at his door and make dying of hunger gestures," Alex laughed loudly and acted some of my actions for Chirag's benefit. Chirag guffawed loudly at this.

While we were talking, a girl came and spoke something to Chirag quickly. Chirag replied and the girl left.

"Was she asking where he is?" I asked, scowling.

"Yeah, poor guy can't walk ten steps straight," Chirag said, chuckling. "These girls are crazy."

"They are," I agreed, feeling really irked.

"But why do you care?" he asked, eyes narrowing with curiosity.

"Because I work with him," I replied simply. "Believe it or not, I actually care about the people I work with. And he's not a bad person."

Chirag raised his eyebrows, "Just not a bad person?"

"Chirag, what do you mean?" I asked, a little too defensively.

Alex, who had been sipping his juice, chimed in, "He is very handsome, isn't he?"

"Why else do these girls keep falling on him?" I scoffed. "You would think that Seoul doesn't have any more handsome men!"

"Handsome and rich!" Chirag laughed.

And I pressed my lips. Of course, CJ was rich! He was the head programmer of the entire ZenTel, I am sure he was a multi-millionaire at the least.

"Good thing he has you to protect him," Alex said with a smirk.

"Whatever," I rolled my eyes. "I'd do the same for you two if girls were randomly falling in your arms too."

That made both of them burst out laughing.

"Well, until you guys don't mind them falling in your arms," I rolled my eyes.

"I won't mind, that's for sure," Chirag chortled. "But are you sure he doesn't like it?" Chirag pressed. "I mean, the guy's popular and these girls would do anything for him."

"I don't think he does," I said honestly, the comment pinched me more than it should. "He always seems uncomfortable."

"But are you sure?" Chirag asked again, giving me a knowing look.

"I..." I started, but then CJ returned and slid into the seat opposite me, making Chirag go quiet.

CJ said something in Korean, his expression puzzled. I understood it as 'What are you saying?'

"I was saying..." I responded instinctively, and suddenly all heads turned to me.

"What?" I asked, shocked.

Chirag gaped at me, "You understood Korean?"

"Umm... I got what he meant," I shrugged, trying to play it cool but I felt uncomfortable. Because I didn't understand what that girl had said to Chirag, I had merely guessed it, however, I understood what CJ had said.

To move on from this sticky moment, I asked, "CJ, do you like it when those girls pretend to stumble and fall into your arms?"

CJ scrunched his face in visible discomfort and let out a huff.

"See?" I looked triumphantly at Chirag. "Told you he doesn't like it."

"He didn't say no," Chirag muttered.

CJ glanced at him sharply and said in his charmingly broken English, "I... a... no like. Thanks for... a... help me."

I couldn't help but chuckle at that.

"See?" I beamed. "I told you," I winked at Chirag but somehow felt CJ didn't like it.

Finally, it was Saturday, a quiet day for me to catch up on a lot of things. I arrived at office a little later than usual. Still, I was surprised to find CJ already there, engaged in what seemed like a very heated conversation over the phone, which was drifting out of his slightly ajar cabin door. He was gripping a stress ball tightly, his voice sharp, filled with frustration. I couldn't understand a word, but the tension in his tone was unmistakable.

Quietly, I took my seat, unable to supress a smile that always flickered on my lips in his presence. Feeling happier than I had anticipated, I fired up my laptop and the screens. The movement, maybe the illuminating screens, caught his attention, and our eyes met.

A calm washed over him almost instantly. His expression softened, his grip on the stress ball loosening. Though he continued talking, his voice had lost its previous edge.

Dropping my gaze from his face, I focused back on my work, soon getting lost in it.

"What are you doing here on a Saturday?" his voice rang out, startling me, not because he spoke, but because his English was so fluent this time.

I smiled, noticing the tablet that was now strapped to his left arm.

"Working," I replied. "What about you?"

"Working," he answered, mirroring my response.

"Why are you not out in Seoul, sightseeing?" he questioned, his tone filled with curiosity.

"Not much of a sightseeing girl," I sighed. "I had a question yesterday, but you were away. Can you help now?"

Instead of answering, he came over and looked at my screen, but after a brief pause, he asked something else.

"Why not a sight… err… girl?"

"You mean, sightseeing girl?" I corrected, amused.

He nodded.

He was standing so close that, for the first time, I noticed a small device tucked behind his right ear. A subtle blinking light caught my attention. Was he hard of hearing?

"I'm here to work, aren't I? Plus, I don't like going out alone. I feel…" I stopped abruptly, realizing I had almost revealed too much.

CJ stared at me for a moment, as if trying to decipher my unfinished sentence, but instead, he turned his focus back to my screen.

We worked in silence until my phone rang.

"Excuse me!" I muttered and walked a few steps away, answering the video call through my headphones.

By the time I returned, I was smiling, feeling lighter after speaking to my kids.

CJ must have noticed. He pointed at the framed picture on my desk and asked, "*Nammae*?"

"Sorry?" I blinked, confused.

He sighed, shut his eyes for a brief moment, and then tapped his forehead lightly as if frustrated with himself.

"Brothers and sisters?" he tried again.

I had placed the photo of my family on my desk on my very first day here, and just like Chirag and Alex, CJ had assumed the children in it were my siblings or relatives. But while I had let the others believe that, I couldn't bring myself to lie to CJ.

"No," I answered, picking up the frame and running my fingers over it lovingly. "Children. This is my family."

His brows furrowed in disbelief, "*dangsin janyeo*?"

I pointed at his lips. "Korean," I reminded him, knowing exactly what he had asked.

"Your children?" he rephrased, his voice laced with shock.

"Yes," I nodded.

He pointed at Dhriti in the picture. "And this?"

"My sister."

"Sister? Not… a… partner?" he asked, eyes narrowing.

"No, not partner. Sister," I chuckled dryly. "She is my sister."

"You married? Husband?" he looked worried.

"No husband," I replied evenly. "I adopted these kids when I was very young."

His entire posture relaxed at that. In fact, his entire demeanour shifted.

"Your parents?" he asked next, his voice quieter.

"Dead," I exhaled, my fingers tightening around the frame.

"Anyone else?" he asked so sincerely that I could not help but answer him with all honesty.

"No one," I answered, my voice soft. "They are all I have," I whispered.

He was silent for a moment before asking, "No boyfriends?"

The way he looked at me, so intensely, it made my breath hitch for a second. But then…

I burst out laughing.

"What?" he asked, genuinely confused.

"I'm raising a family of five on a single salary. You think I have time or energy for a boyfriend? Or that any man would be interested in me when I come with this…" I lifted the photo with a wry smile "baggage?" I finished. I hated this term 'baggage' but in the context, it deemed best.

CJ's gaze turned sharp, "Your family not baggage," he stated firmly. His eyes flicked down to his tablet, reading the translation. "I am proud of you. Supporting them, giving them a home… I am very proud of you."

Something in his voice made my heart clench. I swallowed past the lump in my throat and shook my head.

"Don't be," I whispered.

"Why?" he asked, his brows drawing together.

I hesitated before murmuring in Hindi, my voice barely above a breath.

"Kyuki, tumhe sach pata hota to tum mujhpe fakra nahi, mujhse nafrat karte." (Translation: Because if you knew the truth, you would not be proud, instead you would hate me.)

I didn't expect him to understand. But the moment the words left my lips, his entire expression changed. His dark eyes locked onto mine, intense and unreadable. And then he said, *"naneun neoreul miwohal su eopsda. hal suman issdamyeon, neoreul saranghal ppuniya."*

And just like that, he stood up and left.

Frowning, I quickly scribbled down what he had said and pulled up Google Translate.

The moment the translation appeared on my screen, I felt my chest tighten.

I turned, staring after him, my eyes stinging with unshed tears.

Because my screen read:

"I can't hate you. If I could do anything, I would love you."

10

A walk, a touch, a promise

We worked together the entire day. CJ received numerous calls, which he took from his cabin, but otherwise, he remained beside me, silently working. However, funniest thing happened when CJ suddenly ducked under my table, hiding. "What?" I spoke in alarm but he just placed his finger on his lips and pointed at the entrance of the room.

The room in which we worked was just a small section of the entire floor and it was always guarded. And currently standing at the door, just behind the LOC (Alex and I called that point 'Line of Control' i.e. LOC because no one was allowed to cross it except for a chosen few) was a girl, looking around. Her main focus was on his cabin, which of course was in darkness right now because CJ was hiding under my table!

She spoke something to me in Korean but I didn't understand.

"No Korean, sorry," I replied simply.

She glared at me and asked, "Mr Choi?"

"Mr Choi is not around," I shrugged.

She muttered something but her gestures were clear, so I just said, "No, he is not here."

And tutting loudly, she left.

CJ sighed and sat back properly on the floor.

"Umm, isn't it dirty?" I asked, looking at him relaxing under my desk.

He brushed his hands and laughed. *"Gomawo,"* he spoke, still chuckling and said something more. Which I somehow understood. "Did you mean, thanks for saving you from her?" I asked.

He nodded, looking impressed.

And while he was impressed, I was shocked. Because until yesterday, I had always relied on Alex to translate whatever CJ was saying, but now, without Alex, I could mostly understand him, especially when he spoke about non-work matters.

Was this what the driver had meant by the 'Language of Love'? The thought flickered through my mind, but I quickly brushed it away.

CJ came out of my desk after some time and we resumed work, though, there was something more informal between us. Our conversations were lighter, our arguments were more like banter, and there was something unsaid between us, I guess saving him from a crazy fan would do it!

Normally, CJ left around 5 PM, but today, he stayed.

"I have to go now," I informed him at 7 PM.

"Okay," CJ nodded.

I quickly locked my laptop, gathered my things, and left for dinner. But thirty minutes later, I was back as there was simply too much to do.

As usual, the office floor was shrouded in darkness when I returned. But the moment I flicked on the light above my desk, he reappeared.

He looked perplexed. My heart, on the other hand, jumped into my throat. *He was still here…!*

"What are you doing here?" I asked seriously, placing my bag on my desk.

"I was about to leave but came back as the lights flickered back on," he read from his tablet.

"Oh," I murmured, a strange sense of disappointment settling in my chest. "Goodnight then," I greeted, settling back into my seat to work.

But instead of leaving, he joined me.

"Why are you back?" he read from his tablet.

"To work. I always come back after dinner to work," I informed him.

He blinked but didn't reply.

"You always leave around 5, so you wouldn't know, would you?" I added.

Still, he offered no response. Instead, he simply continued working beside me.

Around 9 PM, he ordered some food, which he ate quietly while we worked. He offered it to me, but I was already full.

"Don't you have to go?" I asked around 11.

"Work from home, work from here, same thing," he shrugged.

"You're allowed to work from home," I pouted. "I'm not allowed to. Hence, I have to spend hours and hours on this hard seat!" I complained.

"You don't like chair? We change," he offered in his cute broken English, his expression laced with concern.

"Nah! I just get tired sitting all day, that's all," I said, stretching my arms. "Anyway, thirty more minutes, then I'll leave too."

He nodded. Then, just before midnight, we left together.

"How do you go home each day?" he asked seriously.

"A security guard accompanies me," I replied, walking towards the security desk. The guard there jumped to his feet upon seeing CJ and saluted him.

"Wow! Never seen him do that before," I chuckled.

"Mr Choi," the security guard addressed him, before launching into rapid Korean.

CJ responded and then gestured for me to step outside with him.

"Umm…" I hesitated, confused.

"I will walk you to the guesthouse tonight," he offered, leading me toward the cycle stand as I unlocked my bike.

"You don't have to," I mumbled.

"But… I… a… want to," he said, this time without checking his tablet.

A blush crept onto my face, my heart thrumming with excitement. I nodded.

"So, who do you have in your family?" I asked as we walked together.

"Family? Mom, Dad, Grandparents," he replied.

"No siblings?"

"No," he said simply.

"Girlfriend? Fiancée?" I asked casually.

He chuckled, "No, no one…"

"Why?" I asked, genuinely curious.

"What why?" he asked, his brows furrowing.

"Why are you single?" I asked bluntly.

He looked at me strangely before shrugging. "Don't like… any… a… girl," he said in his usual broken English.

I found it odd but didn't push the subject. I knew for a fact that the girls here practically drooled over him… how come he didn't like any of them. Some were incredibly beautiful!

"Why don't you like any girl?" I asked, despite myself.

He pouted with a small smile, but didn't reply.

"Here I am," I said as we reached the guest house.

"Here you are," he huffed, turning to face me.

"Priya," he spoke, swallowing hard.

"Yes?" I asked, my voice softer now.

"I…" he hesitated. "I walk you now, okay?" he finally said.

"You want to walk with me every night?" I confirmed, taken aback.

"Yes," he nodded.

"Why?" I was confused.

"Because…" but he stopped short. "Goodnight, Priya," he whispered, lifting his hand to gently caress my cheek.

A shiver ran down my spine. Electricity coursed through me at his touch, and I instinctively closed my eyes. Because in that one small touch, it felt as if he had said everything that words can't express...

"I will see you Monday, then," he whispered.

I nodded, even as my mind screamed at me to tell him I would be working tomorrow too. But for some reason, I couldn't bring myself to speak.

"Goodnight, CJ," I whispered back.

"Neoreul geuriwohal geoya," he murmured, his hand still resting against my cheek.

"I don't understand," I whispered, my eyes fluttering open.

"Nothing," he shook his head, stepping back.

"Gin ilyoiri doel geoya," he added.

I frowned. "Not funny, you know. What if I start speaking in Hindi?" I teased.

"I always understand you," he stressed.

And then, with a small wave, he turned and walked back toward the office.

I stood there for a moment, frozen in place. Then, quickly pulling out my notebook, I scribbled down the words he had said. He might be able to understand Hindi, which, at this point, I was almost certain he could, but he didn't know that I had a semantic memory bordering on eidetic. I never forgot what I heard or read, and while this language barrier between us had caused a few stumbles, I was slowly piecing things together. Whatever I heard, I remembered.

And whatever CJ had just said to me, I would find out.

11

You have me...

I couldn't sleep that night. Since it was Saturday, I ended up having a long, late-night video call with my family. They were missing me now more than ever, and I promised I'd be home in exactly four days.

And while I was thrilled to see my family again, an inexplicable sadness settled over me. Four whole days without seeing CJ! The thought was ridiculous, so I brushed it aside and focused on my family.

It wasn't until the next morning, over breakfast, that I finally got around to translating CJ's parting words.

But just as I was about to do it, Ha-yoon slid into the seat beside me.

"What was Mr Choi doing with you outside last night?" she asked, her voice laced with curiosity.

I almost choked on my food.

"What were you doing up around midnight?" I shot back.

"I have to lock up, you coming late has ruined my sleep," Ha-yoon sighed dramatically, shaking her head. "So? What was happening between you and Mr Choi?"

"Nothing," I replied quickly. "We were working late, and he walked me back."

"Then why did he touch your face?" she pressed.

My hand instinctively flew to my cheek, to the exact spot where CJ's fingers had lingered the night before.

"Right there!" Ha-yoon exclaimed excitedly. "See? I even took a picture."

She pulled out her phone and flashed the screen at me. My stomach dropped… there it was. A crystal-clear image of CJ cupping my cheek, my eyes closed, his expression unreadable.

"Oh god! You clicked a picture?" I gaped at her as I took the phone from her hand.

"Oh, yes. Nothing exciting happens here these days," she sighed. "You and Mr Choi are the hottest thing that's happened in a while."

I stared at her. Hottest thing?

"I'm so sorry!" I gasped, pressing my hands over my mouth. "I accidentally deleted it."

The moment the words left my lips, she shrieked so loudly that the entire dining area turned to look. She switched to rapid-fire Korean, scolding me like a mother whose kid had just broken her favourite vase. I only caught a few words, but I got the gist.

I picked up my empty plate just as she screamed, *"Oneul bam neo jeonyeok eopseo. Manyak eolgul naemilmyeon, naega jikjeop dok tajul geoya."*

I was planning to ignore her, but then the chef behind the counter caught my eye. He made a slicing motion across his throat and whispered lowly, "Poison you. So, eat out today."

"What?" I blinked, stunned.

He nodded solemnly.

Glancing back at a still-fuming Ha-yoon, I decided to take his advice.

I got to the office around 10AM and dove straight into work. I spent a good thirty-minutes chatting with my family, laughing and catching up.

At around 1 PM, Chirag called, inviting me out for lunch. I politely declined. My to-do list before flying home on Thursday was insane and I couldn't afford a break.

Then, at 6 PM, another call came in.

"Where are you?" a voice demanded.

Even though I hadn't saved CJ's number, I knew it was him.

"Who is this?" I asked, smiling to myself.

He huffed, then said, "This is Choi Mirae-Jun."

"I know it's you, CJ," I laughed, tapping away on my keyboard.

But instead of replying, he hung up.

Strange!

Ten minutes later, he pulled a chair beside me.

"What are you doing here?" he asked, his brows furrowed in concern.

"Working. What else?" I smiled, still typing away.

"But why?" he reached out, gently grabbed my hands, and turned me toward him.

"I have no one here and nothing else to do," I shrugged, staring at his fingers wrapped around mine.

"You have me," he said after a pause.

My heart skipped a beat. What did he mean by I have him? How did I have him? And like what?

"I mean…" I scrambled for words and then blabbed, "Chirag asked me out for lunch, but I said no. Too much work, you know."

CJ's eyes darkened slightly, like they always did whenever I mentioned Chirag. "So, you're saying no to me too?" he read from his tablet, one hand still wrapped around mine.

"You didn't ask me anything," I pointed out.

"I went to the guest house before," he said suddenly.

I groaned.

"What?" he asked, confused.

"Ha-yoon took this last night," I sighed, pulling out my phone and showing him the picture.

"Nice picture. Send me?" he asked, staring at us together on my screen.

"That's what you want? A photo? Ha-yoon took this," I stressed.

"She has this now?" he demanded, taking my phone and starting to click through it.

"I sent it to my number and then deleted it from hers. So, she got mad. She absolutely lost it. She even threatened to poison me if I ate there again."

CJ's eyes widened. "Poison you?" he asked grimly.

I laughed, "I am sure she was exaggerating. But yeah, I think I'll eat somewhere else for a few days."

"Nah," he said. "Let's eat in the guest house, together."

I shook my head. "No, I don't want to cause a scene. Your presence… tends to create a scene."

"I know," he smirked.

"Why is that, by the way?" I asked, narrowing my eyes. "What's so special about you?"

"Is there nothing special?" he asked, tilting his head.

"Well…" I hesitated. "At first, I thought you were the owner or something of ZenTel…" I bit my lip.

"Really? But then?" he asked, clearly amused.

"But then I saw Mr Choi, you know the old Mr Choi," I wrinkled my face at the name, "mistreat you, which I still think was very unfair and you should raise it with someone," I snapped. He chuckled, so I added, "Well, so I think, you clearly are not his son or whatever…"

His face fell for a moment, but then he grinned again. "So, nothing special about me?" he asked seriously.

"I didn't say that. I mean, you are special," I spoke hastily. "I mean, you're very handsome," I added, blushing.

His grin turned smug, and my eyes fell on his lips again.

"And… you have such red lips," I added, staring at them. "How do you have such red lips?"

CJ's grin widened. "My lips are a secret," he chuckled.

"Maybe one day you'll share that secret with me," I mused.

"Well…" he leaned in slightly, "Let's see how dinner goes tonight. Maybe I'll tell you later."

Then, without warning, he shut my laptop.

"Gaja, bap meogeureo. Wae achimbuteo gulmeun neukkimi deunya?"

I didn't understand his words, but his intent was clear.

"Let's eat, yes," I nodded.

"You understood?" he raised an eyebrow.

"Not exactly, but I got the gist," I chuckled.

"I said," and he pulled out his tablet and translated, "Let's go and eat, then. Why do I get the feeling you haven't eaten since breakfast?"

My stomach grumbled in response.

"That's true," I admitted sheepishly.

CJ shook his head with a small smile. "Let's go then."

And together, we walked out, hoping against hope that Ha-yoon wouldn't actually poison me.

12

Lines blurring between us

I entered first as CJ was busy on a call and found Ha-yoon sitting in her usual spot. She was scribbling something in a ledger, probably balancing the books, but the moment her eyes landed on me, she started jabbering in rapid Korean.

"I don't care who comes to find you, but I will keep my word and poison you if you ever decide to eat here again," she threatened, jabbing her pen in my direction.

"Who came to find me?" I asked innocently.

"You think you're very smart…" she trailed off abruptly because CJ entered behind me and spoke something in Korean.

Ha-yoon practically jumped out of her seat and bowed so deeply that for a second I thought her nose would touch her knees.

"Mr Choi," she greeted, then continued jabbering in Korean.

CJ responded with something sharp, his tone firm. Ha-yoon spared a disgusted glance in my direction before her expression quickly changed into a wide, forced smile. She laughed awkwardly and muttered something under her breath.

"It was a joke, Priya, a joke of course," she said, waving her hands in mock innocence.

"Didn't sound like a joke to me," I muttered under my breath but forced a smile anyway.

She led us toward a table, but CJ, ignoring her, took my elbow and guided me toward a corner table instead. He said something to Ha-yoon, which I assumed meant we'd be eating here, then dismissed her entirely.

I exhaled, impressed. "Wow! Why is everyone so scared of you?"

"Are they?" he asked nonchalantly but winked nonetheless.

"Yes! Like you're the boss or something," I narrowed my eyes. "Who are you really?"

He smirked as he spoke in his tablet and read the translation. "I am head developer in ZenTel, who are you?" he sipped his water, amused.

"I am a nobody," I shrugged.

He narrowed his eyes, "Not a nobody, no…!" Continuing the routine of speaking in Korean and then reading from the tablet.

I stared at him, shocked, and then he added in a whisper, "A nobody cannot swear about Mr Choi in front of me, or well, challenge and argue with me about anything and everything," he laughed, and I blushed.

Many heads turned as he laughed.

"I don't argue about everything," I whispered, embarrassed now.

"Oh, you do!" he laughed again. "I have never seen anyone do that. People just always agree with me, whatever

I say. It is actually quite refreshing to have someone so smart and bold."

I didn't know what to say! So, I just stared at my hands.

"Hey!" he whispered even softly now. He moved his hands a bit closer to me, so that our hands were slightly touching. "Don't stop challenging me, okay? I like it!"

I nodded, my eyes fixated at our barely touching hands.

Our food arrived shortly after. CJ served me first before filling his own plate, an action that made my heart flutter unexpectedly.

"How do they say in English..." he thought for a moment before grinning, "Dig in!"

Laughing at his accented English, I did just that. As we ate I noticed Ha-yoon sit in the table close to us, and I knew she was eavesdropping, so we didn't talk much after that.

"Care for a walk?" he asked after we finished.

I glanced at my watch, it was just past 10 PM.

"Sure," I replied, "just give me a sec," and I quickly fired off a text to Dhriti, letting her know she could call me as soon as the kids were free.

As we strolled further from the guest house, I persisted. "Now, tell me about yourself."

"What do you want to know?" He turned to me, his expression unreadable.

"Why is everyone so scared of you? And why does no one ever challenge you?" I demanded.

He thought for a moment, then read from his tablet, "Maybe I have that kind of personality," he shrugged.

I scoffed. "I don't think you have a scary personality. You're actually really nice," I laughed.

He arched a brow, "I am?"

"You are. And I have no idea why everyone is so terrified of you, like one wrong move and you'll fire them all," I giggled.

"I don't know," he shrugged again.

"I mean, you have a reserved table in the cafeteria," I pointed out.

"I do, yes," he nodded.

"And no one dares sit at your table."

"You're always there with me," he said smoothly.

"That I am," I admitted, feeling warmth creep up my cheeks.

"And so are your friends," he added, though I could tell he wasn't a fan of them.

"Alex and Chirag are my only friends here," I said quietly.

CJ stilled, then reached out and took my fingers in his. "And me?" he asked softly, "What am I?"

My heart skipped several beats. "My friend too, I guess," I whispered, my voice barely audible. A strange current passed between us, something unspoken but deeply felt.

Trying to distract myself, I blurted, "Are you related to Choi Man-Young?"

He immediately dropped my fingers. "Why do you ask?"

"He's the owner of ZenTel, and I know how he treated you the other day…" I pointed out.

"I remember, yes," he said, completely uninterested.

"But you're also a Choi," I stressed.

"It is a very common name here, Priya," he said, as if I didn't already know that. There were more Chois in my email inbox alone than I could count.

"So, there's no real reason for anyone to be scared of you?" I pressed.

Just then, my phone started ringing.

CJ smirked. "No. And why don't you take your call while I handle some work? Then we'll head back," he read from his tablet quickly.

I narrowed my eyes as I stared at the tablet strapped to his left hand, "Your translator translates surprisingly well, you know. Like, really informal English."

He grinned, "It is because it is not Google Translate. It is my own translator," he read from his tablet, then added with pride, "I design it all," he gestured toward my phone.

My jaw nearly hit the floor.

Still reeling from that revelation, I answered my call. Realizing I had left my headphones back at the guest house, I moved a little to the side for privacy, talking to each of my family members. And for the first time, I wondered, what would it feel like to call CJ my family too?

13

The chapstick conspiracy

Time flew by, and before I knew it, Thursday had arrived: the day of my flight back to India.

That week, much like before, CJ disappeared around 5 PM, only to return after dinner at 9 PM to work with me. And, as always, he made it a point to walk me back to the guesthouse just before midnight. We were getting closer, more comfortable with each other. So comfortable, in fact, that after lunch, he casually handed me a chapstick.

"What is this?" I asked, completely baffled.

"Secret of my red lips," he grinned.

Shocked but undeniably smitten, I just pocketed it. And knowing my habit of losing things from my pockets, I quickly transferred it into my bag the moment I reached my desk. That turned out to be a good decision because, later that evening, I found myself ambushed in the washroom.

I had never seen the bathroom so crowded before, so I decided to use another one. But just as I turned, they spotted me.

"Wait! Wait! Come in, please," one of the girls, who looked a little different from the others, called out.

I hesitated, instinctively wary of a bathroom full of strangers.

"I am Zoey," she introduced herself, offering me her hand. And I recognized her as one of the girls who had tried to stumble in his arms in the past. In fact, most were the girls who roam around him to gain his attention.

"Hi," Zoey spoke again, and I focused back on her.

"I am Priya, hi," I replied, shaking it.

"Can you please show us the chapstick that Mr Choi gave you this afternoon?" Zoey asked bluntly.

Wow. No small talk, no 'how are you' just straight to business.

"What?" I blinked, confused.

"Yes, we all have been dying to know what he uses to get such good lips," Zoey added. One of the girls beside her pouted dramatically, making an exaggerated kissing face. The entire group erupted into giggles.

"Did she just say she wants to kiss CJ?" I asked Zoey, suddenly feeling oddly territorial.

"CJ?" Zoey's eyes narrowed.

"Mr Choi, I mean," I corrected quickly.

"You call him CJ?" Zoey raised a suspicious eyebrow.

Before I could answer, the kissy girl muttered something, and I caught the words *'eye nyeoneun'*, which I knew loosely translated to 'this bitch.' It was enough to make my blood boil.

I shook my head, done with this ridiculous interrogation, and turned to leave.

But the girl kept talking. And that was it.

I whirled around, eyes blazing.

"First, *eye nyeoneun* to you too," I snapped, watching as their eyes widened. "And second, don't worry, I won't tell *CJ*," I stressed his name deliberately, savouring the way they flinched, "that you all cornered me in the bathroom, demanding to see his chapstick."

Before they could react, I turned on my heel and walked away, now more determined than ever to find a different bathroom, because, honestly, I really needed to pee.

Two flights of stairs down, I finally found an empty washroom. But as I stepped out, I nearly slammed into him.

CJ was here.

It was 6 PM, the first time I had ever seen him around at this hour.

"What you doing… here?" he asked slowly, tweaking his ear in a way that seemed almost…nervous? Weird. But I let it slide.

I scowled instead; the bathroom encounter still fresh in my mind.

"Come back with me upstairs and take back your damn chapstick," I growled.

"What?" he laughed. "Why?"

"A gang of girls cornered me in the upstairs bathroom, demanding to see your chapstick," I huffed.

He considered my words for a moment. And then, to my absolute irritation, he burst into laughter.

"You're laughing?!" I snapped. "I am absolutely pissed off! I barely understood half of what they were saying, but their faces, oh my God!"

"Faces?" he asked, his amusement still evident.

"They looked like they all wanted to kiss you!" I blurted out angrily.

CJ stiffened, glancing around nervously, then ran a hand through his hair.

"I not kiss them," he said firmly. "Never."

I froze. Something about the way he said it, so seriously, made my stomach flip.

"I know," I muttered and then continued angrily, "But honestly, these girls just drool over you. I mean, you're handsome, yes. And you have such lips, oh God, it's a crime to have lips like yours," I threw my hands up dramatically. "But why do they act like you're a celebrity or something?"

He shrugged. Like it didn't even matter.

"You're not a celebrity or something, right?" I asked suspiciously.

"No, am not!" he insisted. And then, after a pause, he added, "My lips? Crime?"

I rolled my eyes, just realizing how I had spoken my mind without any filter. "Oh, you know what I mean."

But he only looked more amused.

"Anyway, come upstairs, take back your chapstick, and then no one will bother me. Alright?" I turned toward the emergency staircase.

"I… a… meetings," he followed, and stopped me after a few steps with a gentle touch to my arm. "I go back."

And, damn it, his broken English was way too cute.

I tilted my head, studying him. "How do you understand everything I say but struggle to say it back?"

He smirked.

"But, don't – be – angry – those girls – nothing, nothing, okay?" he said, stressing each word carefully.

"Who said I'm angry?" I barked, crossing my arms.

And he chuckled. A deep, rich chuckle that did dangerous things to my heart.

Then, he did something unexpected.

He placed his index finger against his lips and asked, "This crime?"

My gaze immediately dropped to those perfect, ridiculously kissable lips.

And in that moment, the only thought in my head was: not kissing those lips would indeed be a crime.

As if he had read my mind, he leaned in.

A feather-light kiss landed on my left cheek, making my knees wobble dangerously.

He pulled back and stared at my face, as if reading my reaction. But I was shocked, too shell-shocked to even react. But he must have noticed that I didn't mind it.

So, he bent again and kissed me firmly this time on the same cheek.

I sucked in a sharp breath, my heart thudding heavily now. And though some kisses don't reach your lips… they still manage to leave your whole world trembling. And that's how I felt in the moment.

"Later, talk later," he whispered, so close that his breath fanned across my skin, sending a wildfire of shivers down my spine.

And just like that, he was gone.

14

Bogo Sipeosseo

In my daze over what had just happened, I had completely forgotten that I had a flight that night. After all, it was my first kiss which had made me feel something. I was still sitting on the staircase, replaying the moment in my head, when my phone started ringing. It was my driver, Mr. Jong.

Reality came crashing back, and realizing the time, I hurried up the stairs, waved a quick goodbye to Alex, who looked thoroughly puzzled at my flushed face and dreamy expressions, and rushed off with my bag.

It wasn't until I was in the air, after switching off my Seoul phone and turning on my Indian number, that I realized I hadn't informed CJ about my departure. A pang of guilt hit me. But considering he was the one who had approved all my travels and stipends, I assumed he already knew.

I was incredibly excited to meet my family, but for the first time, something felt... off. It was an unfamiliar ache, one that refused to go away, no matter how much I tried to shake it off. I missed him. More than I should. And the worst part? I missed him more than I missed my own family.

I spent four wonderful days with my family. The kids flat-out refused to go to school on Friday and Monday, and we had an absolute blast together. Every single day, we went out, visiting different places in Delhi, relishing the carefree freedom of being home. It was a much-needed break from staring at a laptop screen all day.

Dhriti, ever the thoughtful one, had bought some gifts for the kids from a local shop upon my suggestion, and we spent our nights playing with them, laughing like children ourselves.

During those four days, my phone rang incessantly, Ashok, my boss in India, clearly hell-bent on reaching me. But I ignored every single call. This was my time. My family's time. And I wasn't going to waste it, especially by talking to someone like Ashok, who was bound to spoil my mood.

But even amidst all the joy, a certain someone never left my mind.

CJ.

I missed him every second of every day. I hated how much I did. I hated the guilt that came with it, the way my heart clenched at the thought of him. Dhriti, being the perceptive sister she was, noticed my dilemma and tried to ask me multiple times. But each time, I avoided the question.

What was I even supposed to say?

That I had fallen head over heels for a man I'd only known for ten days? That a simple, fleeting kiss had left me in such a daze that all I wanted was to hide in his arms forever?

I wasn't that naive. I knew it was just a crush, a ridiculous, intense, completely impossible crush that would come crashing down in exactly two months and fifteen days.

Because no matter how much I felt for him, he wasn't important enough for me to leave my family. And I was certainly not important enough to him to ask me to stay.

I flew back on Monday night, reluctantly switching gears from 'home mode' to 'work mode.' But before I boarded, I used that time to call Ashok while I waited at the terminal.

To say he was furious was an understatement. He was livid.

"You ignored my calls for four days, Priya! Four whole days!" he barked the moment he picked up.

I sighed. Here we go.

"You called me fifty times, Ashok," I pointed out dryly.

"Damn right, I did! And you didn't have the curtesy to pick up the call even once?" he snapped.

"My phone was silent," I lied.

There was silence for a few seconds, and I knew Ashok was trying to reign in his temper.

"I was this close to busting down your door…"

"Oh, so you came over," I muttered. Figures!

"Of course, I did! But no one was home. Where the hell were you?"

"Out with my family. You know, like normal people do when they visit home?" I replied simply.

He let out a frustrated huff. Then, after a beat, he said, "Mr Choi called me."

That caught my attention.

"He did?"

"Yes," Ashok's voice turned suspicious. "And he didn't say much. Which makes me think… Did you do something in Seoul that made him call me?"

My mind immediately flashed back to the kiss.

I cleared my throat. "I didn't do anything," I said, forcing my voice to sound as normal as possible.

"Then why did he call me?"

I swallowed. "I have no idea. I thought he was happy with my work."

"I want answers. Call me the second you check with him," he ordered.

"Sure," I said, already regretting this entire conversation.

As soon as I hung up, my frustration morphed into excitement.

Because tomorrow I was going to see CJ again.

Stepping out of the Seoul airport, I scanned the crowd for Mr. Jong, my driver. But instead, my heart lurched into my throat as my eyes landed on someone else.

CJ.

He was standing there, hands stuffed in his pockets, eyes locked on mine.

I grinned instantly. But his expression? Dead serious.

Without a word, he stepped forward, grabbed my suitcase, and started walking toward the parking lot.

The silence stretched. Thick. Heavy. Unsettling.

It wasn't until we were seated in the car that he finally spoke. And when he did, it was rapid, furious Korean.

He didn't stop. Not for breath. Not for anything. At one point, he even pulled at his hair. I sat there, stunned, unable to catch a single word.

But I didn't need to.

I got the gist.

"…are you upset and angry that I left without informing you?" I asked cautiously.

He shot me a sharp glare.

Okay. That's a yes.

"But you should be aware of my travel arrangements," I reasoned. "After all, you approved my travel budget."

He huffed.

Ah! "Okay, so you approved the budget, but not the itinerary?"

He nodded furiously.

I bit back a smile. "Let me guess. You only found out yesterday?"

The fiery look in his eyes confirmed it.

I chuckled. "You were worried for me?"

His nostrils flared.

"You were very worried for me, I see," I teased.

More rapid Korean.

This time, I reached out, placing my hand over his on the steering wheel and squeezed it lightly.

And in that moment, I noticed something.

My hand: tanned, lined, a little rough.

His hand: smooth, flawless, almost unfairly perfect.

The contrast made me hesitate. I pulled my hand back, suddenly feeling self-conscious.

"I had to visit my family," I said softly. "I'm fine, CJ."

For the first time since we met today, his anger flickered.

"I thought… you ran away," he murmured. "That I… a… kissed you… and you ran away."

I turned to face him fully.

"I didn't run away, CJ. I'm not stupid," I sighed. "And can we drive now? I have a lot of work, you know."

But he didn't move.

Instead, he said something so soft, so unexpected, it sent my heart into overdrive.

"Bogo sipeosseo."

I blinked.

Fumbling for my phone, I quickly typed it in.

My breath caught at the translation.

'I missed you.'

I stared at him.

And in that moment, I knew he meant it.

I wanted to tell him that I missed him too, but I didn't. Instead, his words reminded me of two more lines he had said before, last Saturday when he had walked me to the guesthouse, which I never got to translate.

So, I picked out my dairy from my bag and translated them too,

"Gin ilyoiri doel geoya" – It's going to be a long Sunday.

"Neoreul geuriwohal geoya," – I will miss you.

15

Turning the other cheek

We drove in silence, with CJ glancing my way every other minute. I had no idea what was running through his mind, but whatever it was, it couldn't be anything ordinary.

What was happening here? I had never been the centre of anyone's affection… like, ever. Once, six years ago, I had a boyfriend at ZenTel. He told me he loved me, but he made it clear he wanted no responsibility of my children. And honestly, I didn't blame him. Who would willingly take on the responsibility of not just one, but three children and a sister? I had broken up with him after only two months of dating, despite liking him a lot. He had moved away soon after, and I had learned my lesson the hard way.

But was I about to learn an even harsher lesson now? I was falling, fast and hard, for CJ. And the worst part? We weren't even from the same country. How could this possibly work?

"What are you thinking?" CJ asked as he pulled up outside the guest house.

"Nothing," I lied, shaking my head.

"I will wait for you. Go and get changed," he ordered, eyes glued to his tablet.

"I'll take some time. You go ahead, please," I requested.

He studied me for a long moment, then nodded. I hopped out and tapped on the trunk of the car. He opened it. I pulled out my bag, and without a second glance at him, I turned and walked inside.

I took my time freshening up and then called home. Dhriti and I talked for a while before I stepped out of my room to grab a quick snack from the kitchen. Ever since that Sunday when CJ had dined with me, Ha-yoon had been acting surprisingly cool towards me. She had granted me full access to the kitchen, something strictly forbidden for guests, and allowed me to eat whatever I wanted, whenever I wanted.

"He came to pick you up?" she remarked as I took a bite of an apple.

"Yes," I sighed. Of course, she had seen me stepping out of his car.

"And he brought an Aston Martin," she chuckled. "He must be trying to impress you!"

"Aston Martin?" I echoed, confused.

She gave me a suspicious look. "Don't tell me you didn't notice what he was driving."

Honestly? I hadn't. I had been too focused on *him* to pay attention to what he was driving.

"I don't care about cars," I said simply.

"You *would* notice if he were driving a Kia Ray," she eyed me knowingly.

I had no idea what a Kia Ray was, and I didn't care. I sighed and walked out, only to find CJ still sitting there, working on his tablet.

I hesitated, standing there for a moment, but he didn't look up.

What was I supposed to do? I didn't want to get attached to him, but the way he was acting, the way he was treating me, I *knew* he was going to break my heart into a million pieces.

Taking a deep breath, I walked toward him. This time, I actually noticed the big Aston Martin logo on the car.

I knocked on the window, and he looked up.

"Why did you wait for me?" I asked simply.

"I got a call, couldn't leave," he replied as I sat beside him.

I nodded, accepting his answer at face value.

"You have a nice car," I commented, feeling like I should acknowledge it.

"You *just* noticed?" he chuckled.

"I only noticed because Ha-yoon pointed it out. Otherwise, I wouldn't have," I shrugged.

"She does notice such things, yes," he nodded.

"Yeah, she's funny and weird," I agreed.

"That she is," he said, sounding oddly formal.

It irked me. I wanted to close this distance between us, but I didn't know how, or even if I should.

"What is Kia Ray?" I asked, glancing at the endless traffic. We could have reached the office *four* times by now.

"A car," he looked confused. "Why?"

"Ha-yoon said I'd notice if you drove a Kia Ray," I pointed out.

He laughed, "I don't drive Kia Ray."

"Why not?" I asked, genuinely curious.

"It is, well… a *very cheap* car," he said.

Something in his tone rubbed me the wrong way. A cold, sharp feeling of humiliation crawled over me. Fine, he was rich… much richer than most people… but did he really think *poor* people were beneath him? People like me?

Mistaking my silence, he pointed at a car nearby and said, "That's a Kia Ray."

I looked at it and smiled. It was exactly the kind of car I had always dreamed of buying when I had enough money. The *only* kind of car I could ever afford.

"And driving that car would humiliate you?" I asked, my voice sharper than I intended.

"Hum – what?" he looked confused.

I grabbed his tablet that was sitting in the gear box and typed 'humiliate'. The Korean translation, *changpireul juda*, popped up on the screen. I pressed the small mic button, and the robotic voice spoke it aloud.

CJ hit the brakes so suddenly that the car behind us honked furiously. He started ranting in rapid Korean.

"Oh, just get out of the road, will you?" I sighed.

I could swear he cursed under his breath before pulling the car to the side. Then he snatched the tablet from my hands and jabbered into it again. Moments later, he shoved it back at me.

I read:

"I am not humiliated or embarrassed by anything or anyone. I am not ashamed to walk or even ride a cycle with you. I have my comforts, yes, but that doesn't mean I'm spoiled or a snob. When I said it was a cheap car, I meant in terms of money, not that it was beneath my standards. So please stop misunderstanding me!"

I blinked.

"Can I have a tablet like this?" I asked seriously.

He glanced at me, a small smile playing at his lips now.

"Why?" he demanded as we finally reached the office.

"Because it is so easy to carry and handy. It will help me survive here," I shrugged.

He nodded thoughtfully as he parked right at the main entrance and handed his keys to the guard standing there.

"I thought everyone parked downstairs?" I asked, frowning.

"I get special treatment," he shrugged, taking the tablet from my hands.

"Why?" I demanded as he led me toward the staircase instead of the elevator.

"Because I am the head coder," he winked. And somehow it made sense. He coded everything that ZenTel sold, so he was, indeed, very special.

"Are we climbing *five floors*?" I groaned, looking up.

"No," he sighed. Then, without warning, he stopped at the landing and turned to me. "I just want to do this."

And then, just like that, he pressed his lips firmly against my *other* cheek.

I stood frozen. My mouth hung open.

"I thought you left because I kissed you," he read from his tablet. He was standing so close to me that our body was practically merging into one. "But since you didn't, I figured you left because your *other* cheek was upset. So, I've made it even now," he whispered, his breath raising havoc all over my body. He kissed me again on the same cheek, and then once more.

My eyes were bulging out of my sockets now with shock. What was he even doing?

A smirk tugged at his lips as I instinctively covered my right cheek with my hand.

"We can take the elevator now," he grinned, grabbing my hand and pulling it away from my cheek. Then, without letting go, he led me toward the elevator.

16

A note left behind

Things stayed very much the same that week, except for a few notable changes. For starters, that afternoon, Chirag cornered me, his face set in a deep frown as he scolded me, rather angrily, for leaving without informing him.

And only at his words I realized that I had been so absorbed in my work, and well, CJ, that I had missed telling anyone and everyone that I was going back!

"Mr Choi went berserk when he didn't find you that night. He called everyone, demanding your whereabouts, and when Ha-yoon informed him that you had taken a taxi and left with your luggage, he nearly lost his shit. I have never seen him, or well, anyone, so devastated," he said, his voice edged with frustration.

I was speechless. What was I supposed to say to that? There was nothing between CJ and me, nothing except a few stolen kisses, that too on the cheek, nothing more than that! And let's not forget, he was Richie-rich, and I was beggarly-poor.

"What is going on between you and him?" Chirag asked seriously, his sharp gaze fixed on me.

"Nothing. I think he's just protective of me because, you know, I'm here to develop that tech he's betting so much on," I replied honestly. It was the truth, he had bet against the world on this revolutionary tech, something that could change the face of the mobile industry forever. And that's why it was so secretive, so high-stakes.

"Maybe," Chirag said, though he didn't sound convinced. "But he was freaking out like his girlfriend had left him."

At the mention of the word 'girlfriend,' something inside me jolted, an involuntary reaction I hated myself for.

Chirag must have caught the flicker of something on my face because he sighed and added, "Listen, Priya, he's charming and all, but he's up here," he stretched his arm to its fullest height, "And we're down here," he brought his hand down to his knees. "We are nothing in comparison. Having feelings for him will only break your heart, okay?"

"I'm not the one running around worried, Chirag," I shot back, feeling a little stung by his words.

"That's true, but he has girls lined up after him. You're different. You're new, so he's feeling some fondness for you. But please, take note… our worlds are very different. He's up there," he repeated, stretching out his hand again. "Be cautious of him. And also of his fan following, because believe me, if the word got out that he's even slightly interested in you, there would be hundreds of girls within these offices alone lining up to push you down the stairs."

Worried for my safety, and not willing to be labelled as whatever the Korean equivalent of 'sl^t' was, I decided to keep a safe distance from CJ.

But it was evident that he had no such intention.

No matter how much I tried to bring others into conversations or route things through Alex, CJ always found ways to talk to me. And even though I stayed glued to Alex or Chirag during office hours, CJ always managed to find me alone, because every single day, he walked me to the office, and then back to the guesthouse.

And somehow, I both dreaded and cherished those stolen moments in his company.

And, without fail, each day, we climbed at least one floor through the stairwell. And every single time, he would stop midway and press a series of kisses on my cheek, my forehead, or sometimes, my hand.

I liked it the most when he kissed my forehead. It gave me a sense of... completeness. A feeling of being seen, cared for.

And they were just kisses, simple kisses, they were not even passionate or anything more, but somehow, they became my world. And he became my favourite place to belong…

But they were wrong.

All of it was wrong.

And I knew I needed to put an end to it before things escalated beyond control. Because the most beautiful things are often the ones that break you the hardest. And he was the most beautiful thing in my life at the moment…

That Saturday, just like before, I left for the office. And there he was again.

Waiting.

Standing beside one of his many cars. We never drove in cars anymore. He arrived each morning in his car and left it in the guesthouse. And then walked with me.

I had long since given up on keeping track of how many cars he owned. But today, as I walked toward him, I wondered why did he keep bringing a different car every day? Was it a show-off thing? But he must know by now that I wasn't into materialistic things.

As I stepped out, he tossed the car keys toward Ha-yoon, muttering something under his breath, just like he did every morning. Then, he fell into step beside me, walking in silence.

I had decided. Today was the day. I was going to confront him. This had to stop.

But before I could get a single word out, his phone rang, and he swore, or at least, that's what it sounded like.

He answered and immediately started jabbering in rapid Korean. I couldn't understand a word, but I could tell he was upset.

For the first time since I came back, we didn't take the stairwell.

And he didn't kiss me.

Instead, we took the elevator, and he went straight to his cabin, his brows furrowed, his entire focus on whoever he was arguing with on the phone.

And despite deciding to put an end to this whole 'kissing' train, I felt oddly empty.

Everywhere he had kissed me these past few days ached and burned, like my body missed his touch.

And that day, I don't know what had happened, but he never touched me again.

Saturday passed. Sunday came.

He dropped me off at the guesthouse on Saturday night. But in the morning, he didn't come to pick me up.

I walked to the office alone, feeling the weight of something I didn't want to name pressing against my chest.

A note sat on my desk.

"I am traveling. Will be back soon."

No details. No explanation. Just a message.

How soon? He didn't say.

Monday came and went.

He left a ton of instructions for me and Alex to follow, along with an absurdly long to-do list.

But he didn't show up.

I saw him very briefly on Tuesday, but he was so busy that he didn't even have a second to spare me a smile.

Chirag, who found it weird sitting at his special table in the cafeteria without CJ there, dragged me over to his other friends.

Soon, I started socializing with them, or, well, as much as I could given the language barrier.

It was strange. With CJ, I normally understood the gist of what he was saying, despite the language difference. But with others, I barely understood a single word. Chirag had to translate everything.

Wednesday blurred past.

And finally, Thursday arrived, the day I was leaving for home.

And despite all my reservations, all my worries, all my tension about our status quo… I just wanted to see him once more before I left for four whole days.

But he wasn't there.

The whole day passed, and he didn't return.

So, before leaving, I scribbled a small note and placed it on his desk.

"I'm leaving for India. Will be back on Tuesday. Hope to see you then."

And with an incredibly heavy heart, with a pain I never thought I would feel for any man ever, I left for the airport with Mr. Jong.

17

Forbidden and Unspoken

After passing through immigration and security check, I called home. Deep down, an unbearable loneliness gnawed at me, so I did what I always did in such moments, I reached out to my family, the only people in the world who were truly mine.

I was talking to my kids when I reached the boarding gate and then I stopped dead in my tracks.

Pacing up and down, checking his watch incessantly, was CJ.

For the first time ever, I disconnected the call abruptly.

I swallowed hard and approached him. The moment he saw me, he rushed forward, his body tensing as if he was about to hug me, but at the last second, he stopped himself.

"Hi," he said.

"Hi," I whispered back.

"I was waiting," he sighed.

"What are you doing here?" I asked, my voice firmer than I felt. "I don't think visitors are allowed post..." I gestured behind me toward the security check, but he just grabbed my hand and led me aside.

"Don't worry about that," he smiled.

"But how? Did you buy an international ticket or break some rule?" I pressed, my concern growing. Neither scenario sat well with me.

"Don't worry about it," he repeated, flashing me that same frustratingly easy-going smile. Then, suddenly, his hands cupped my face, his fingers gently squeezing my cheeks, like I was some kid he found adorable. "Ah…" he cursed softly, glancing at his watch. "Thirty minutes before you go," he murmured, the words laced with regret. "Can we talk, please?"

I nodded. We sat on a bench at the side, and he exhaled heavily.

"*Bogo sip—e—o—ss—e—o*," I spoke awkwardly, trying out the Korean words I had picked up.

His eyes widened.

"*Bogo sipeosseo,*" he corrected, a strange emotion flickering across his face.

I nodded.

"I missed too you," he whispered. "You learn Korean?"

I smiled at his English. He was trying so hard for me, so I was trying too, even if just a little.

"Trying… catching a few words you say," I admitted.

He grabbed my hand and squeezed it.

Then, pulling out his tablet from his jacket pocket, he spoke rapidly into it before handing it over for me to read.

"I have been forbidden to see you."

My eyes widened.

"By who?" I demanded.

He spoke into the tablet again, and I read the next words.

"I have been trying to be discreet. I even changed cars, but somehow, word reached him. And he forbade me."

"Him who? Your father?"

He nodded grimly and spoke into the tablet again.

"I don't care about him," I read, my stomach tightening, "but he brought my mother into it. I love her, I respect her, and he made her ask me to stop seeing you. And I always listen to her."

Chirag's words echoed in my mind. 'Our worlds are very different. He is there.' I instinctively looked up, as if trying to see where CJ's world really was. And yes, it was true…we were different. Worlds apart.

"I understand," I said, my voice barely above a whisper. "If you believe me, last Saturday, when you picked me up from the guesthouse, I wanted to talk to you. I wanted to ask you to stop."

"Stop?" CJ's eyes narrowed.

"Kissing me," I murmured so softly that he had to lean in to hear me.

"Why?" he asked, his voice low, warm, right near my ear, raising goosebumps all over my skin.

"It's unfair to both of us," I admitted, trying to keep my voice steady.

"Meaning?" he asked, eyes narrowing further.

"CJ, we are very different," I sighed, and he just stared at me, waiting. "I know why I'm attracted to you, I mean, you're just perfect. But I don't understand… why do you like me?"

He blinked rapidly, clearly thrown off.

"Why I like you?" he repeated, confused.

I nodded. "I mean, look at me," I laughed hollowly.

"I am looking. Yes," and as he said it, I saw something in his eyes… affection. Not shame. Not disgust. Not the way I felt about myself.

"How can you even like what you see?" I spoke abruptly, harsher than I meant to. "I'm pathetic."

He grabbed my hand and squeezed it firmly.

"You are pitiful?" he asked, puzzled.

"No," I shook my head, "pathetic. It means ridiculous, worthless, absolutely low standard…"

His brows furrowed, eyes darkening.

"You make me anger," he hissed. "You not that…" he snapped.

I just closed my eyes and shook my head.

He tapped on his tablet, directing my focus to it. As I looked at the screen, he began jabbering in Korean – rapid, sharp, almost like he was scolding me.

"You call yourself worthless," it read, "but to me, you are important. No one stood for me against Choi Man-Young. But you were ready to jump in when he insulted me. I never asked you, but you just knew how much I hate when those girls jump on me. You've been making sure that doesn't happen again. I know you've made enemies of those girls, but it doesn't matter to you. You only care about me."

He paused for breath, glaring slightly at me, more emotionally charged than angry.

"I heard you that day, you said you'd do the same for anyone else too… While I'm not a fan of that part," he added, half-smiling, "I like special treatment. But it shows how sincere and honest you are. You make sure I eat. You make sure I'm not harassed. Believe me… no one has ever done that for me!"

He paused for a moment, then spoke, "And you… you make me mad when we work… but that's exactly what I want. People who challenge me, not just do whatever I say. If I only wanted obedience, I wouldn't need experts from Europe or India here, right?"

I swallowed hard, stunned by the force of his words.

"And when I kissed you, you didn't jump on me… Any other girl would have laid down then and there, but you… you felt it. Like you… like you…" he stopped. I looked up at him, and in his eyes, I saw what he meant. I had felt every second of it, just like he had.

I was speechless.

"Don't insult yourself, okay?" he whispered, reaching out to touch my cheek, gentle and affectionate.

I looked in his eyes, my face warm, and nodded faintly.

"But… you're here, in Seoul. My life is back in Delhi. We have our priorities. Us getting close won't help anyone. And… I do understand your parents' concerns," I said softly, almost reluctantly.

He exhaled sharply and stood up, suddenly restless. He ran a hand through his hair in frustration.

"Jeohui eomeonineun dangsineul bandaehaji anayo," he muttered under his breath, almost angrily.

"What?" I frowned. "Korean!" I reminded him, blinking.

He cursed lightly under his breath and then spoke into his tablet again before handing it to me.

"My mother is not against you. In fact, she respects you for taking in three orphans and caring for them at such a young age."

I flinched at the word orphans, but I said nothing.

"She even said she's proud of you. That you are kind and compassionate, not like the girls who hover all over me all the time," he added bitterly.

"Why do girls hover all over you?" I asked, casually… but I had wanted to ask it for a long time.

And just like that, he laughed. A real, amused, carefree laugh that lit up his whole face.

"Naega uri eommaga neoreul injeonghandago malhaneunde, geuge geokjeongdwae?" he smirked.

I frowned. "Did you just say, your mother approves of me and yet I'm still worried about other girls?"

He grinned, thoroughly impressed.

"Well, of course," I scoffed. "I know I've been saving you from them, but I want to know today, why do girls hover all over you?"

He thought for a moment, then smirked. "For my criminal lips," he said, making an exaggerated pouting expression.

And despite everything, I laughed.

After a beat, I sobered. "So… your mother has a problem with me being Indian?"

He immediately shook his head.

"Then what is it?" I asked, more seriously now.

He hesitated. "Promise me you won't be upset?"

I gave a small, grim smile, "Whatever reservations she has, I probably deserve them. Just tell me."

He exhaled, then winced slightly before answering, "Your age."

I blinked. Of all the things he could have said, that was the one I never saw coming.

"I know it's not a big deal," he added quickly, "but you are three years older than me. And that's a big concern for my mother. They're very conservative. They believe a man should always be older than his wife for a happy marriage."

I swallowed hard. Wife? I should have been focused on the rest of what he said, but that word '*wife*' echoed in my mind.

"You're twenty-nine, right?" I asked, carefully.

"I'll turn twenty-nine in a few weeks," he said easily, completely unaware of the storm those simple words had just stirred inside me.

"And I will be…" I started, mentally calculating.

His eyes narrowed, "Thirty-two. In three months."

I nodded sadly, "That is true, as per my official birth date."

He frowned at my wording, "As per your *official* birth date? Then how old are you *really*?"

I opened my mouth to answer, but just then, the boarding announcement echoed across the terminal. I stiffened. I couldn't believe I had almost told him.

"I have to go," I said, standing up.

"Next Saturday is my birthday party," he said suddenly. "You're invited."

Worry crossed my face. What will I wear?!

"There's a theme," he smirked, reading my expression too easily. "I'll tell you what to wear."

I nodded hesitantly.

Then, his hands cupped my face. "Don't worry. Even if you wear your office clothes, you'd still be the most beautiful girl there."

Goosebumps erupted all over me as I read his words on the tablet. I knew he was lying… I had never been *the most beautiful girl* anywhere, but I smiled anyway.

The air hostess called again.

"Can I hug you?" he asked softly.

I shook my head. I wanted to, but if I let myself get closer, I didn't know how I'd ever pull away.

He sighed, "Fine. Maybe later."

But then, just before I could move, he grabbed my hand, pulled me close, and kissed my forehead, deeply, lingeringly.

And despite myself, I placed my hands on his back.

"This is a hug, right?" he murmured against my skin.

"Ma'am, Sir, you need to board now," the air hostess interrupted.

CJ swore under his breath and handed me a new boarding pass.

"I already have mine," I said.

"I upgraded you to business class."

"What?!"

"Safe flight," he smirked, poking my nose.

"Seriously, who *are* you?" I demanded.

"I am CJ," he grinned. "Call me from India. I'll wait."

And then, with a heavy heart, I walked away feeling strangely empty because he had held me close enough to make me forget… and then let me go, reminding me I never really had him.

18

Learning to say "I Miss You"

CJ was truly spoiling me. The luxury of traveling in business class was beyond me. I had never even dreamed of it. But I enjoyed it nonetheless.

And throughout this comforting journey, a thought kept nagging at the back of my mind… who exactly was CJ?

I suspected he was related to Mr Choi Man-Young, the owner of ZenTel, but CJ had outright denied it. Why would he lie to me? I wondered. But considering I had never told him the truth about myself, I could hardly blame him, could I?

I decided that once I was back home, I would thoroughly Google CJ. And if he chose to be honest with me, I would do the same. I would tell him my truth. Starting with… well, everything.

I spent the next four days fully dedicated to my family. But unlike last time, we couldn't go out or do much. Dhriti and Dhara, our eleven-year-old, were both ill, running high fevers and coughing relentlessly. And I was absolutely helpless.

Dhriti could barely sit up straight… how would she take care of the kids, the house, and herself in my absence?

So, despite her insisting that she would manage, I called CJ. Ideally, I should have called Ashok first, but… I didn't.

The moment he answered, he said something in quick Korean.

"Umm, hi, I don't understand Korean," I smiled despite the situation. His voice alone had that effect on me.

"Wait!" he said quickly, then added, "I have been waiting for your call for three days, you know!"

And I had been dying to call him. But I had held back. I had ignored him completely. Yet, what I couldn't ignore was the ever-growing emptiness that crept in every time he crossed my mind, which was every waking second.

He had started starring in my dreams around fifteen days ago, but now, it felt like my dreams were no longer mine, instead they belonged to him. It was like a movie where he was the lead hero, and I was just another fangirl, lamely trailing behind.

"Bogo sipeosseo," his words pulled me back to reality.

"Bogo sipeosseo," I replied. I had been practicing saying 'I miss you' in Korean in private, to be honest in the bathroom.

"Nice!" he laughed. "So, what's wrong?" his tone shifted, firm and concerned.

"How did you know something was wrong?" I asked, surprised.

"Because you're supposed to fly back today, and yet, here you are, calling me. I'm sure you wouldn't have if everything was fine," he sighed. "So, what happened?"

"My sister and daughter are very unwell. I don't think I can come back yet," I admitted solemnly.

"Ever?" he asked, too quickly.

"Not forever, just this week, maybe," I sighed. "I'm sorry. I know you spent a fortune on my tickets and everything but now, I…"

"Enough!" he cut me off. "Not worried about the money here."

"No, I know you'll have to answer to someone… I'll pay you back… umm…" I hesitated and then added, "eventually!" Because we both knew I couldn't pay him back anytime soon.

He tutted so loudly that I had to pull my phone away from my ear.

"First," he hissed, "I don't care about the money. And… wait!" I heard him tapping his tablet, likely translating. "And I don't answer to anyone. People answer to me!"

"How? I mean, why?" I asked, puzzled.

"Not important," he dismissed. "But I don't answer to anyone, Priya. So don't worry about it, alright?"

"That's not true," I countered, remembering the conversation with Mr Choi in the cafeteria.

"Wait!" he muttered something in Korean. "Why don't we do a video call?" he suggested. "I haven't seen you in days, and I don't know when I will see you again."

"I don't…" I started, feeling epically self-conscious about my unruly hair and my lower-middle-class home.

"Now! Calling you now," he said, disconnecting the voice call. A second later, my screen flashed with a video call invite.

I had been talking to him from the kitchen. Now, I rushed to the balcony before answering.

"Hi!" I greeted the moment his face appeared.

"Hi back!" he grinned. "This is better."

"It is," I admitted, attempting and failing to smooth down my flyaway hair.

"So, you were saying?" he prompted. "What's not true?"

It took me a moment to remember, then I said, "Oh! You do answer to someone."

"Really?" he challenged, tilting his head. "Who?"

And considering he always got upset when I referred to Mr Choi, I digressed, "Your mom," I grinned, rolling my eyes.

And he burst out laughing.

"Yes, of course! She is my mother. I answer to her. I love her."

His words made me smile.

"Though…" he paused, his eyes gleaming mischievously. "I think I'm starting to answer to someone else too."

Goosebumps erupted all over my arms. But bracing myself, I asked, "Really? Who?"

"There's a girl," he teased, smirking. "I'll introduce you to her some time."

And just like that, my heart plummeted. He met another girl.

"Can't wait!" I forced a smile, pulling myself together. Of course, it was good that he had met someone. I could never be that girl for him. I was… well…

"So, when are you coming back?" he asked, turning serious.

"I don't know," I sighed. "They're really unwell. And I'm sorry I'll miss your birthday party."

"Ah, don't worry about the party. I'll push it," he dismissed.

"But it's your birthday," I argued.

"Nah, my birthday isn't on Saturday. The party was…" he shrugged, "so I'll just push it to when you're back."

"So, when is your actual birthday?" I asked, curious.

"Not this Saturday," he grinned. "Wait," he picked up another phone, called someone, spoke rapidly in Korean, then hung up.

"*Appa* wanted me to go to London this week. I said no. So, I will go now. How about you come back after that?" he suggested.

"Appa, as in your father?" I asked.

He nodded with a smile. I wanted to ask who he was, but I resisted. Instead, I asked, "You're going to London?"

"Yes, duty calls," he sighed.

"Why did you say no before?" I asked seriously.

He narrowed his eyes and then read something from his tablet. "It hurts me to know that you even have to ask!"

And just like that, I was speechless.

"So, you can take a break until your family is fine. After that you work from India office," he spoke, still reading from his tablet. I nodded, feeling a sudden wave of sadness.

"However, I have two conditions," he added after a pause.

"Two conditions?" I echoed.

"You have to do a video call with me when you wake up, right from bed, before you go to sleep, before you start work, and after you finish work," he ordered.

My eyes widened in shock. "Four video calls?"

"Yep!" he nodded vigorously. "I cannot go without talking to you or seeing you for days."

My heart grew heavier at his words.

"CJ, that's not practical," I whispered.

"That is my first condition," he insisted.

"What if you're busy?" I asked, hoping to reason with him.

"Then I will call you back, and you have to answer," he stressed.

"I can't call you from bed. I don't sleep alone, you know," I said, reluctantly giving in.

"Who is in your bed?" he demanded.

"My sister and my daughter," I replied.

"Ah, then it's fine," he laughed.

I narrowed my eyes. "Who did you think?"

"No one," he shrugged.

"Who do you think would be in my bed?" I demanded.

He grinned mischievously. "I can think of someone who might join you in the future."

And my heart sank.

"No one can join me in my bed in the future except for my sister, CJ. Don't mistake that, please."

His lips thinned, but he didn't argue.

"Fine, you can call me when you get out of bed, but you have to call me first thing in the morning. Deal?"

"Deal," I nodded. "What's the second condition?"

"I'll ask Alex to continue working on the prototype in our absence. I will, of course, guide him. But you cannot work on the prototype from India," he stated firmly.

I nodded again. That was expected.

"So," he grinned, "I want you to fulfil your number of days and extend your trip by, let's say, twenty days in exchange for this break."

I gasped. "Twenty days in exchange for ten? Unfair, isn't it?"

"All's fair in… well, my company, my rules," he shrugged.

I raised an eyebrow, "Your company?"

He paused for a moment, then added with a smirk, "Well, I am the head programmer here. If I don't develop, this company will tank," and then he blew raspberries to prove his point.

I burst out laughing, an unrestrained, genuine laugh. His eyes twinkled at the sound.

"Neomu bogo sipeo. Dasi neoreul nae pume aneul nareul gidaril su eopseo," he spoke huskily.

"*Nado bogo sipeo,*" I replied, pouring as much love as I could into my words. "And whatever you said afterward, that too," I grinned before rushing inside to scribble his words on a paper, determined to remember them exactly.

He raised an eyebrow.

"What? I've been practicing saying 'I miss you' in various ways," I laughed.

"Good job," he chuckled.

"Goodnight, CJ. And… thank you," I said softly.

"Joeun bam doeseyo, my Priya," he smiled.

I blinked. "Isn't 'goodnight' just '*Jal ja*' in Korean?" I asked, confused.

He laughed. "It is, but what I said was 'Have a good night.'"

"Oh, God!" I groaned. "How will I ever learn this language?"

His smile turned teasing. "I have a few suggestions… but let's park that conversation for the future."

"*Jal ja,* Priya."

"Goodbye, CJ," I whispered before disconnecting.

19

Between love and family

"You have fallen in love with someone, haven't you?" Dhriti asked between her coughs that night. Dhara was fast asleep, and both the boys were tucked away in their room.

"Love?" I scoffed, shaking my head.

"You met him barely a month ago," she pointed out, her brows furrowing in confusion.

"Exactly," I nodded, folding my arms.

"I don't love anyone except for my family, and you know that," I stressed, hoping she'd drop the topic.

Dhriti's eyes softened, but she didn't let it go. "You know we just want you to be happy," she murmured, her voice strained. I couldn't tell if it was emotion or her health making her sound so fragile.

"I *am* happy, Dhriti. Here, with you all," I sighed, running a hand through my hair.

"I saw you talk to him," she continued, studying me carefully. "I have never seen you smile and laugh like that before. Not like this… *never*," she said softly, and the sadness in her voice made my chest ache.

I swallowed. "I like talking to him, yes," I admitted.

"You're happy with him," she didn't ask… she *stated.*

I let out a slow breath. "Does it even matter?" I finally asked.

"Why?" Her voice was barely above a whisper. "Because you feel stuck with us?"

I snapped my gaze to her. "I am *not* stuck, okay? You are my family. I would never do anything to jeopardize that," I said firmly.

Her eyes filled with tears as she whispered, "I want you to be happy, but…"

"But *what*?" I prompted, feeling my stomach twist.

"I'm sorry, but I can't let you go and be with him," she choked as tears streamed down her face. "I mean… I've always been terrified that one day you'll find someone and leave us."

My breath caught. "What are you talking about?" I demanded, completely thrown.

"You go out every day, you meet people. I stay home… I have no chance of being with anyone," she sobbed. "And I'm scared, scared that one day, you'll leave us behind."

I blinked at her in disbelief. "You *honestly* think I'd do that?"

"My only solace," she continued, her voice breaking, "is knowing that you will *never* leave Rohan and Dhara."

And then it hit me.

She wasn't afraid of me moving on… she was afraid of being left *alone.*

I exhaled sharply. "And you think I'd take Rohan and Dhara with me and leave you and Dhruv behind? Are you out of your bloody mind?" I nearly shouted. "You *actually* think Dhruv is not my son?"

"I'm sorry," she sobbed. "I got so scared when I saw you talking to him."

"Dhriti," I murmured, pulling her into a tight hug. "You and the kids are my priority. Nothing… *nothing*… will ever change that. CJ is my friend, and yes, I enjoy talking to him. But he is not for me. He is just intrigued by me, no one falls in love that easily. He met me and is fascinated. And that's what it is, a fascination, mere infatuation. What I have here with you is love. I love you and our kids. Please don't insult me by thinking I would choose a guy over you. And don't *ever* dare to think that I would leave you." I pulled back slightly, looking her dead in the eyes. "Because the *only* way I'd ever leave you is if I die."

She broke into fresh sobs and hugged me even tighter.

Of course, she was scared. If she fell for someone, I would be scared too.

"We made a promise to each other ten years ago, Dhriti," I said seriously, wiping her tears away. "I will always honour it. And if I *do* end up with someone, he'll have to accept the full package: five people for one." I grinned, and finally, a small laugh broke through her tears.

She sniffled and scrunched her nose playfully. "So… you couldn't have fallen for an Indian guy? I mean, I saw him… he's *very* good-looking, but *still!* Korean?!"

I chuckled, twisting her nose lightly. "It doesn't matter whether he's Korean or Indian. Men struggle to handle women as it is. And we come with a whole *baggage* no man can deal with," I smirked. "So… let me have some fun while it lasts."

Dhriti sighed, shaking her head. "Just make sure your heart doesn't break in the process."

I laughed at her words, but deep down, I knew the truth.

My heart was already broken.

CJ and I? We could never be.

So, I will cherish him until it lasts… because, ours was a love, that could never last.

20

A battle of power and control

I stayed home for two more days before rejoining the Delhi office on Thursday. The moment I stepped inside, Ashok's face darkened, his expression twisting with rage. His jaw clenched, his nostrils flaring as his sharp gaze locked onto me. Without a word, he flicked his fingers, gesturing for me to follow him into his office.

"What are you doing here?" he demanded the moment I shut the door.

I took a deep breath and explained my home situation, and how CJ (though I made sure to refer to him as Mr Choi in front of Ashok) had offered me a fifteen-day break.

"And you didn't bother to ask me? Didn't even consult me before deciding this?" his voice rose, his fury barely contained.

"I was very stressed, and considering I was working with…"

But he cut me off with a thunderous shout, so loud that a tense silence settled over the office outside his cabin.

"I don't care what your reasons were! You are in my team. Your work reflects on me, on my reputation. Just because they've asked for you, you think you can do as you please?" he scoffed, shaking his head. His tone was venomous, each word sharper than the last.

"You didn't even tell me why Mr Choi was asking for you when you last came back to India. I had explicitly asked you to inform me after discussing with him, but you think so highly of yourself that you forget who your seniors are. Have you forgotten who you are? What I've done for you?" his voice turned cutting, a cruel smirk playing on his lips. "If I can make your career, I can break it too," he flicked his fingers dismissively. "I give you so much leeway…" and then he continued, venting his pent-up frustration for what felt like an eternity.

It was as if he had been holding back his resentment for years, waiting for this exact moment to unleash it all. He dredged up every tiny mistake I had ever made, right from when I was a clueless intern eleven years ago. I couldn't believe he remembered all that. And for what? Just to belittle me?

Tears welled in my eyes and spilled over, flowing unstoppable, unchecked. My vision blurred as I stared at the floor, humiliated and exhausted.

My phone rang, breaking the suffocating parade of insults.

Ashok's head snapped toward me, his expression darkening further.

I quickly reached for my phone, about to disconnect the call, when he barked, "Who is it?"

"Mr Choi," I sniffled.

His demeanour changed in an instant.

"Why is he calling you?" he asked, his voice suddenly measured, almost cautious.

"To discuss the prototype, why else?" I answered, my voice barely steady.

"Answer him," he ordered.

I looked at him, still blinking away tears.

"I cannot like this," I gestured at my tear-streaked face.

"As if he cares. Just answer him," he sneered, his patience wearing thin.

Scared that he'd start shouting again, I hesitantly accepted the call.

Ashok's face visibly stiffened as he realized it was a video call.

"H – " CJ had just begun with a warm smile when his expression shifted instantly. His eyes narrowed, his voice sharp as he asked, *"Museun iriya? Wae ulgo isseo?"*

I swallowed hard. "I am fine," I choked out. I knew he was asking why I was crying?

"Wae ulgo isseo?" he repeated, more demanding this time.

"Are you asking me why I am crying?" I sniffled.

"*Dangyeonhan geo aniya? Geuraeseo mureobon geoya!*" His words came out so fast, so forceful, that this time, I barely caught a single one.

"Here, give me your phone," Ashok interrupted, his voice laced with irritation as he gestured for me to hand it over.

I did as he asked.

"Hello, Mr Choi," with a sudden shift in tone, Ashok bowed slightly toward the screen, his expression plastered with forced politeness.

"What happened to her?" CJ demanded, his voice clipped.

"She's just a little upset," Ashok let out an airy laugh, as if dismissing it.

I wanted to punch that laugh right out of him. Instead, I wiped my nose on my sleeve.

"And why is she upset?" CJ pressed.

"Family matters," Ashok lied smoothly.

CJ's tone darkened, "Or you mistreated her?"

Ashok stiffened. "No, sir. Ask her yourself… it's family matter."

And without missing a beat, he turned the phone toward me, giving me a sharp, warning look.

"Yes, family," I nodded mechanically.

CJ wasn't convinced.

"Mr. Tyagi," he spoke, his tone now edged with anger. "Let me call you on your Teams ID."

And he disconnected.

The room fell dead silent.

"Why did you take his call?" Ashok turned on me immediately, his voice sharp.

"You forced me to," I snapped back. "I didn't wish to take it, remember?"

"How was I supposed to know it was a video call?" he gritted his teeth as his laptop started ringing.

He shot me a furious look and spoke, "Come here, explain to him first, and then explain to me later why he was video calling you."

His tone was nothing short of threatening.

I sighed, stepping closer as he answered the call.

Ashok sat beside me, scooting uncomfortably close to get in the frame.

CJ's eyes narrowed immediately. Then, he gestured for me to shift.

I did, just a little.

He gestured again.

I moved further until only half of my face was visible on the screen.

"Maintain distance," CJ ordered, his tone icy.

"Of course, sir," Ashok let out a nervous chuckle.

CJ's gaze flickered to me, then back to Ashok.

"Did he abuse you, Priya?"

Ashok's head whipped in my direction so fast I thought his neck might snap. His moustache twitched violently, his entire face flushing with anger.

I quickly shook my head. No.

But the look in CJ's eyes told me he wasn't convinced.

CJ studied my face, or what was visible on screen, and his expression darkened. He spoke rapidly into his tablet, then glanced at the translation before reading aloud, "Mr Tyagi, mutual respect is very important in ZenTel, and we do not tolerate bullying."

"Bullying…" Ashok began indignantly, but CJ raised his hand, silencing him with a sharp gesture.

"If Priya puts in an official claim, I will fire you. But since she is clearly denying it, which I can see is under duress, I will personally ensure you receive an official warning from HR. I am the witness here, Mr. Tyagi," CJ stated firmly.

"She is upset for personal reasons, sir," Ashok insisted, his voice strained.

"Did something happen at home?" CJ asked me, his eyes softening slightly.

I opened my mouth to say no, then hesitated, and finally gave a weak nod.

CJ spoke quickly in his tablet and read the translation, "We talked barely an hour ago, and you were laughing with your sister," CJ countered, his voice laced with suspicion. "Mr Tyagi, you're not just mistreating your team members, you're coercing them into lying for you. There will be an official inquiry," he hissed.

"Please don't," I whispered to CJ. "Ashok has been my mentor for over a decade. If he scolds me, it's fine. We all lose our temper sometimes," I added, my voice barely above a breath.

CJ huffed.

"Neo ulgo isseosseo," CJ muttered irritably.

"Yes, I was crying, and I cry a lot because that is my life, CJ. You can't punish everyone who makes me cry, alright?" I snapped.

Ashok's jaw dropped at my outburst.

"Whatever may it be, HR will handle this matter, Mr Tyagi. Mark my words," CJ said, his tone final.

I stood up abruptly and turned towards the door.

"And Priya, I will call you in some time," CJ added sharply before disconnecting.

"Wait!" Ashok called out just as I reached the door.

"What?" I whipped around, my patience hanging by a thread. "I just saved your ass, didn't I? You insulted me, berated me for nothing, yet I still covered for you. Enough is enough!" I snapped.

"What is going on between you and Mr Choi?" Ashok demanded.

"Mr Choi – or CJ – is my friend. We are working on a prototype together, and we've developed a friendship, that's it," I said, my tone exhausted.

Ashok's eyes narrowed at my words, his moustache quivering with barely concealed fury. I knew he wanted to say something, but his laptop dinged insistently, demanding his attention. With a frustrated grunt, he dismissed me.

I didn't have much work in the Delhi office since I was fully dedicated to the prototype project, so I decided to focus on finishing my translation agent… the one that would help me communicate more fluently with CJ.

I spent the entire week working on it but hadn't yet tested it properly. So, on Monday, on the morning of my flight to Seoul, I decided to try it out.

I typed out the heartfelt words CJ had spoken to me during our very first video call and waited for my agent to process them.

I entered: *Neomu bogo sipeo. Dasi neoreul nae pume aneul nareul gidaril su eopseo.*

Translation: *I miss you so much. I can't wait for the day when I can hold you in my arms again.*

My jaw dropped at the translation. Was it correct? I quickly Googled it, and yes, it was.

"If you're planning to say those words to Mr Choi, I'd advise against it. Maintain professional boundaries," Ashok's voice sliced through the silence, making me jump.

I spun around, my heart hammering. He had crept up behind me and was reading my screen.

The freak!

"I was building a translation agent," I explained defensively.

"To have an affair?" he demanded.

"No!" I snapped, my temper flaring. "To translate codes in various languages."

"Which code includes 'holding someone in your arms'?" he demanded, crossing his arms over his chest.

"I saw this phrase on a TV show, so I was testing the translation accuracy," I bit out.

"You remember a 'phrase from TV'?" he mocked.

"You know I have semantic memory and I remember everything, whether I read something or hear!" I scowled.

"Are you having an affair with Mr Choi?" he asked outright.

I stiffened, glancing around nervously. Thankfully, we were alone as it was breakfast time.

"No," I said, my voice measured but firm. "He is a friend, a good friend, but just that, a friend."

"Do you know what people call girls who develop friendships with men like Mr Choi?" he hissed.

I raised my eyebrows. "No, and I don't want to know. But what exactly do you mean by 'men like Mr Choi'?"

He huffed, then, as if suddenly remembering the consequences of insulting me last time, he softened slightly.

"I'm sorry," he sighed as he sat on a chair next to me. "I guess I feel… insecure."

"Insecure?" I echoed, confused by the sudden shift.

"I feel like you're pushing me aside, treating me like an afterthought," he said glumly, pushing his chair closer.

I stared at him, shocked.

"I have never mistreated you, Ashok. I have my priorities, and I follow them," I retorted, frustration creeping into my voice.

"I like you, Priya," he confessed suddenly, his eyes locking onto mine.

"What?" I was stunned by his words.

"I always have. You are so simple, beautiful, and how should I say it… I feel so comfortable around you. Why can't you add me to that list of priorities?"

And then he placed his hand on top of mine. My eyes popped open in shock. And while CJ's touch sent pleasant shivers down my spine, Ashok's touch rang blaring alarm bells all over my body.

He was married… or at least, I thought he was.

"What are you saying?" I asked, pulling my hand and pushing my chair back to get some space from him, "You're married."

"We separated months ago," he admitted. "But I guess it's not a priority for you to remember when I told you."

He told me. Really? When?

"I'm sorry to hear that, but I don't have time for any of this, Ashok," I said, shaking my head.

"Yet, you have time for video calls with Mr Choi," he shot back.

His words made me pause. Then, suddenly, I remembered his earlier accusation.

"What was that name you mentioned earlier, for girls who 'befriend people like CJ'?" I demanded.

"CJ?" he repeated, eyes narrowing.

"Mr Choi," I clarified, crossing my arms.

"Well, I thought you didn't want to know," he asked slyly.

"Now I do… tell me," I challenged.

He exhaled sharply, "You tell me, what do you call a girl who befriends only one person in a foreign country?"

"Nothing!" I said impatiently. "Why should there be a name?"

"And what if that one person happens to be one of the richest men in the country?" he countered sarcastically.

"What do you mean?" I asked, my stomach dropping. "CJ is the head programmer at ZenTel, that's it."

Ashok stared at me like I was missing something obvious.

"You do realize he is a Choi," he said slowly, as if speaking to a child.

I felt the blood drain from my face. My hunch… could it be right?

"There are many Mr Chois in South Korea," I murmured. "It's a common last name."

"Yes, but your CJ is *the* Mr Choi."

My heart thundered in my chest. "What do you mean?" Ashok crossed his arms.

"He's the only son of Choi Man-Young," he said, watching my reaction carefully.

My jaw dropped.

"No, I saw Choi Man-Young insult CJ publicly, humiliate him. And CJ said he wasn't related to Choi Man-Young," I blabbered, unable to believe it.

"Many fathers humiliate and insult their children," Ashok said with a shrug, "especially when they shirk their duties and bounce around with random girls."

My blood curdled at his accusation, but his next words stopped me from reacting altogether.

"And no matter what *your CJ* may have indicated, *he is the sole heir to this billion-dollar company.*"

21

A gold-digger in billionaire's arms

This time, when I left home, there were no tears. My kids were fine; they knew I'd be back in ten days. I guess Dhriti had prepared them well. But I had a sneaky suspicion that they weren't exactly counting down the days for me, they were counting down for the presents I'd bring back. Typical kids!

After that revelation from Ashok, I had gone home, bid farewell to my family, and was now making my way toward the boarding gate.

"You are a billionaire, and I am a gold digger," I muttered under my breath, dragging my bag along as I stared at my phone. The words stung. I wanted to confront him, demand answers. Why had he lied? Why didn't he tell me the truth?

"I would not have gotten this close to you if I knew you are that rich. Our worlds don't meet. I am nothing..." I whispered, staring

at the blank screen, trying to formulate my thoughts. How was I even supposed to begin this conversation?

Just as I was about to settle into a seat, two strong arms wrapped around me from behind, holding me tight.

I yelped, my heart leaping into my throat. But then a deep voice whispered in my ear, *"Dasi dangsineul nae pume aneul geunal-i deudieo wasseoyo."*

I exhaled sharply, my body going still. I turned around, and all my questions, my confusion... everything... vanished the moment I saw his face.

He looked exhausted. Not just tired... exhausted. His usually neat hair was dishevelled, his tie askew, and dark shadows clung to his eyes like he hadn't slept in days.

"What are you doing here?" I demanded, concern replacing my shock. "And why do you look like you haven't slept in weeks?"

He pouted, huffing dramatically.

"Dangsineul mannareo yeogikkaji nara watneunde, ireon baneungiranyo?" he muttered.

"One second," I interrupted, pulling out my laptop. I clipped the mic onto his shirt, he looked confused, and placed my headphones on my ears.

"Now, say both sentences again."

He raised his eyebrows.

"Please," I requested.

Rolling his eyes, he obliged. *"Dasi dangsineul nae pume aneul geunal-i deudieo wasseoyo."*

I read the translation on my screen:

"The day when I hold you in my arms again has finally arrived."

I felt warmth creep up my cheeks.

"Okay, what did you say next?"

He hesitated, then repeated, *"Dangsineul mannareo yeogikkaji nara watneunde, ireon baneungiranyo?"*

I read the screen:

"I flew all the way here to meet you, and this is your reaction?"

My jaw dropped.

"But why?" I asked, my concern deepening. "You look like you haven't rested in days."

"I missed you," he sighed, pulling me into another embrace. But I didn't reciprocate this time. People were staring.

"Umm, this is India, CJ. No PDA," I whispered, squirming.

He pulled back, looking around. "So, if I want hug and kiss my *yeo-ja-chin-gu*, I cannot do it in this country?"

My eyes widened at his words. I glanced sideways at my laptop, where the translation flashed on the screen.

"Girlfriend?" I blurted out, blinking.

"Yes," he nodded, completely unfazed. "I decided in last two weeks, you my *yeo-ja-chin-gu*," he tapped his chin against my head affectionately.

My stomach flipped.

"Let go of me," I muttered, wriggling free.

"Or what?" he teased, smirking.

"Someone will say something. And also, I think I'm about to drop my laptop."

He groaned but finally let go.

"So, what is this algorithm?" he asked as we took our seats.

I noticed people still throwing curious glances our way.

"I know your tablet is one of a kind and you need it, so I developed this," I explained. "Now, all I need is a mobile version. Whatever you say, it'll auto-translate."

"That's impressive," he nodded, grabbing my laptop and testing it by speaking random Korean phrases. "It's giving good output. Might need some fine-tuning."

"Of course. Google Translate isn't exactly accurate," I chuckled.

"That's true. Hence, I built my own," he smirked.

I stared at his smiling yet exhausted face. My fingers itched to touch him, to smooth down the crease between his brows, but I resisted.

"So, what are you doing here?" I asked again.

He reached for my hand. "May I?"

I nodded, and he squeezed it tightly, closing his eyes. Then he spoke in Korean, and I read the translation.

"I planned my trip to London so that I could be here today. I wanted to see you sooner, spend time with you and your family. But I had too much work. I talked to Dad, and he understood, but he needed me, so I had to stay."

My chest tightened.

"When was the last time you slept properly?" I asked softly.

"I slept the whole way here," he smirked and yet he was looking so tired! "I arrived five hours ago, ate something in the café outside, and then waited for you here."

"Why didn't you call me?"

"It's fine. I had a lot to finish anyway, so I worked most of the time. That way, I can spend more time with you."

I sighed, watching him. "And before this flight? When did you last sleep?"

He opened his eyes at that, studying me. "Why do you ask?"

"Because you look exhausted, CJ. Like, unhealthy exhausted."

He smiled, then, before I could react, he lifted my laptop between us and pressed a quick kiss to my cheek.

My heart stuttered.

"Thanks," he whispered.

"For what?" I stammered from behind the laptop.

"For caring about me. And if you had permitted me, I would have thanked you properly," he murmured, his gaze lingering on my lips.

I hurriedly put the laptop to my lap again. He sighed, shutting his eyes again.

"Speaking of your dad," I asked, clearing my throat. "What did you tell him?"

"Just that I like a girl and want to go see her," he replied with a smile.

"What is your dad's name?" I asked carefully.

"Park Sang-ho."

I yanked my hand from his grip, glaring at him.

His eyes fluttered open. "What?"

"But you're Mr Choi," I stated.

"Mr Choi is my biological father, yes."

A sudden suspicion gripped me. "And what's your biological father's full name?"

He hesitated, "Does it matter?"

My stomach dropped. "If it's Choi Man-Young, then yes, it damn well matters," I snapped.

He grimaced.

I shot up from my seat, "Oh my God. You are ZenTel," I almost screamed.

"ZenTel is a company, not me," he deflected, waving a hand dismissively.

"You know what I mean! You're the bloody owner of ZenTel."

"Future owner, yes," he nodded carelessly.

"You lied to me," I thundered.

Heads turned in our direction.

"Igeoseul jom deo sajeogin hwangyeongeseo nonuihal su isseulkka?"

I glanced at my screen.

"Can we discuss this in a more private setting?"

I didn't wish to. I wanted to get all the answers right away, but considering how everyone was staring at us, I nodded stiffly.

Silence stretched between us.

And then, under my breath, I muttered, "That's why Ashok called me a gold digger. Because you're a billionaire, and I'm nothing. I am in fact a gold-digger in a billionaire's arms!"

CJ stiffened beside me.

But before he could respond, the air hostess called for boarding.

I made one last video call to my family and walked inside, CJ silently trailing behind.

22
The sleeping billionaire

He was not happy, but he was quiet… dangerously quiet. Normally, people I met in my life wreaked havoc when they got angry, but CJ was the opposite. When he was mad, he didn't explode, he imploded.

Feeling guilty that he came all the way over to India to meet me and I upset him, I tried to make peace.

"Tell me this," I spoke conversationally, testing the waters. "ZenTel doesn't have private planes?"

He smirked.

"So, that's a yes, I guess," I prodded, and he nodded curtly.

"Will I get to travel in it?" I asked, genuinely curious. "Or at least look at it on the inside? I want to see a private plane!"

He gazed at me in amusement.

"Any other wishes you have for the billionaire?" he demanded, cocking an eyebrow.

"Umm, not really," I chirped, ignoring his sarcasm. "But I do wish to visit N Seoul Tower. You know, I've been in

Seoul for a month and haven't seen anything except the guest house and the office," I pouted.

He studied me for a moment, then nodded.

"Anything else?" he asked, this time, his tone a little more serious.

"Umm," I tapped my chin thoughtfully. Then, without thinking, I grabbed his collar, pulling him closer, and whispered in his ear, "And I want to visit the Moon, maybe even Mars, Venus, and Neptune," I chuckled, biting my lip to keep from laughing outright.

He turned to look at me in shock, and only then did I realize how close we were. His eyes flickered to my pursed lips, then moved back up to meet my gaze.

"I can Moon when they make…" he hesitated, then pulled out his tablet, spoke something, translated, and said, "I can book seats on the spaceship when they start commercial trips to Moon."

"Oh my God!" I exclaimed, "I was just joking."

"Joking?" he asked, confused.

"Of course! I don't want anything from you. I'm happy with what I have," I added simply.

He didn't respond, just sat back straight, indicating quite clearly that he was still pissed.

"So, you travelled all the way from London to be with me?" I asked, trying to start over.

"Yes," he nodded, though his voice lacked conviction.

"And yet, you're not talking to me," I huffed, crossing my arms.

He stared at me in disbelief, then shook his head.

"You were right," he sighed.

I looked at him expectantly.

"I am very tired," he muttered as he reclined his seat back.

I blinked. Wait, when did we even take off?

He called the air hostess and asked for a few things.

"What?" I gasped as he pulled a blanket over himself, slipped on an eye mask, and just like that, he was out. Or at least pretending to be.

The flight was seven hours long. Possibly the longest seven hours of my life.

At first, I just stared at him, my mouth slightly open. How could someone sleep so easily after being so angry?

Then I watched a Bollywood flick.

Then I stared at him some more.

I ate, I slept, I drooled over him (figuratively, I hoped), but he just didn't budge. He kept on sleeping.

The only upside to this painfully long flight was that I got a good chance to study his face properly.

Unlike most men I'd seen here, his hair wasn't neatly parted in the centre. Instead, his hair was always combed back, slightly tousled, yet effortlessly perfect.

I noticed three tiny moles on his face. Small, but against his pale skin, they stood out.

And his lips… those beautiful, perfect lips.

About five hours into the flight, when my frustration had finally settled into a dull hum, I felt another kind of itch… one that was a lot more dangerous.

I wanted to kiss him.

But I think kissing a sleeping man, in the middle of a flight, would be considered some form of molestation.

Even if that same man had called me his 'girlfriend' before.

Girlfriend! Geez! Did I even want to be his girlfriend? Or anyone's?

I poked his cheek when we finally landed.

He was now sleeping with his mouth slightly open, his breathing soft and steady.

Adorable.

I clicked a few pictures, regretting not taking more during the flight.

Just as I was about to poke him again, he suddenly grabbed my wrist and murmured something against my arm.

Goosebumps erupted across my skin. A wave of heat spread through me despite the cold surroundings.

"CJ," I whispered, gently patting his face. "We have landed. CJ!"

We were the only ones left in the plane now, and the air hostess was watching us curiously.

"CJ!" I patted his face again. Dear God, how deeply did he fall asleep?

"Is everything alright?" the air hostess asked.

I raised a hand in her direction, a silent 'wait' gesture, then resumed my attempts to wake him up.

He groaned softly, shifting slightly. Finally, some response.

"Wake up, we have landed!" I said, as he slowly pushed his eye mask up from his face and blinked at me blearily.

Still half-asleep, he muttered something, words I couldn't understand.

The air hostess, however, smiled bemusedly.

And then, before I could react, he leaned in and kissed my cheek.

What the – ?!

"Sir, you need to deboard," the air hostess said, her voice tinged with amusement.

CJ nodded, still looking at me. Like I was something important.

Then he stretched, grabbed our carry-ons, and started walking off the plane.

"Thank you for flying with us," the air hostess called from behind us.

I hesitated, then turned to her. A sudden curiosity creeping in.

"What did he say when he woke up?" I whispered.

She glanced back at CJ, then smiled.

"He said, 'You are so beautiful.'"

I blinked. What?

"Really?" I asked, my heart suddenly thudding a little harder. No one had ever called me beautiful before! Well, Ashok did, but he was a creep so that didn't count…

She nodded, still smiling. "You are very lucky."

I turned back to CJ, who was waiting for me just ahead.

And for the first time since this flight started, I was the one who fell completely silent.

23

Let me burn

We stepped outside together, and I immediately noticed a driver waiting with another man, a slightly older gentleman with a warm, paternal smile.

"Saengil chukhahamnida, Mirae," the man greeted CJ, his voice long and drawn out, filled with warmth and familiarity. Then, without hesitation, he hugged him.

As they spoke in Korean, I quickly searched the phrase on my phone, and my jaw nearly hit the ground. Wait… was it really his birthday?

The driver efficiently placed our luggage in the trunk while CJ gestured for me to come closer. As I reached him, he casually draped an arm around my shoulders, his deep laughter filling the space between us. The older man addressed me in Korean, and before I could fumble for a response, CJ smoothly replied on my behalf. They exchanged a few more words, smiles, and nods before the man left with the driver.

"Shall we?" CJ asked, holding the car door open for me.

I hesitated, still reeling from my discovery. "Is it really your birthday today?" I demanded.

"You can wish me if you like," he grinned, effortlessly charming.

I swallowed, suddenly feeling nervous. "Happy birthday, CJ," I said softly, placing a hand on his cheek. "May you have all the love in the world." My voice was sincere, filled with a depth I hadn't expected.

His gaze locked onto mine, intense and unreadable. "That is to be seen," he murmured before gently pushing me into the seat and shutting the door.

The moment we pulled out of the airport, CJ broke the silence. "So, now we talk," he reached over, placing his tablet in my lap, the translation app already open.

I frowned. "About what?"

My English words instantly flashing on the screen. "About what?" it read back at me. Duh! But I knew his words would soon appear there in English too for my benefit.

"Whatever you wanted to talk about yesterday. You see, there are many people who would pay a fortune to know my life story, so I don't share it in public," he said, his tone wry.

"Oh. That..." I trailed off. I had wanted to ask about his family, his status, and most importantly, why he lied to me. But not today. Not on his birthday.

"Yes," he nodded, his grip firm on the steering wheel as he took a route unfamiliar to me.

"Where are we going?" I asked, looking around.

He glanced at me with a smirk, then reached over, grabbing my hand. "We," he said, squeezing my fingers, "are," he lifted my hand to his lips, pressing a soft kiss to my knuckles, "taking a leave today in honour of my birthday."

My heart skipped a beat. Maybe three. We were skipping work? We were going somewhere alone? We were… Oh God!

He exhaled deeply, still holding my hand in his lap. "Before we get there, let me tell you something," he began.

"It's your birthday, you don't need to…" I started, but he squeezed my fingers again, silencing me.

"I asked everyone not to tell you about my parentage," he admitted.

I blinked. "Oh!" Well, what else could I say?

"You have no idea what it's like to be me," he continued.

I scoffed. "You mean filthy rich, not a worry in the world?" I teased.

His expression darkened instantly, and I immediately regretted my words.

"You're right," he finally said, his voice quieter now. "I have money. More than I could ever spend. But I am lonely."

The weight of that single word struck me, squeezing my heart.

"Every girl I meet is trying to impress me. They want what my last name offers, not what I do. They'll do whatever I want… even shed their clothes at a single gesture," he paused, his grip on my hand tightening. "But I want more. I want honesty. Trust."

I swallowed hard, unable to look away.

"You saw how they linger around to gain my attention. But it wasn't you. You were different, so different. When I met you, I knew you had no idea who I was. And I was fascinated. At first, it was your work, I brought you here for my prototype, after all. But then I saw you," his lips twitched. "You, struggling with your chopsticks, completely lost in your own world, and I think… I think I fell for you right then and there."

My breath caught in my throat.

"Then how you reacted to my bio-dad, he insulted me in front of everyone because he wanted to show me my place. That he is the CEO and he has the power, but your indignance on my behalf was, well, priceless," he smiled. "I know you were ready to pounce on him when he was shouting at me, but you stopped on my account, for me… and I really appreciated that. You felt angry for me, and then controlled your emotions on my account," he spoke sincerely. "And I don't think anyone, literally anyone has the guts to use swear words for Choi Man-Young in ZenTel's premises, well, anyone but you," he chuckled and I stared.

"Well," I spoke timidly. "He is not a nice person," I spoke lamely.

"That he is…" CJ nodded, "but you are a very nice person. And you're not fake. You're honest. So damn simple that I…" He stopped, shaking his head. "I have no words for what I feel for you."

I stared at him, my pulse roaring in my ears.

"I didn't want you to see me differently. I didn't want you to treat me with reverence just because I'm your boss. If you had known my truth, our little banters would have stopped. You would have been formal with me. Distant. Just like others. And I couldn't let that happen."

I understood. Of course, I would have treated him differently. I never would have gotten this close. Never would have let myself like him this much.

He was already unattainable, but now… with his wealth and social status… he was like the sun. Something I could admire from a distance, but never touch.

"Say something," he whispered.

I let out a slow breath, "How can I not stay away from you now that I know who you are?"

He pulled the car to the side of the road and turned to look at me fully. Then, with a slow, wicked smile, he simply said, "Because now… you just can't."

And he was right.

No matter how much his light burned me, I knew I would keep reaching for him.

"I really, really, and I mean really like you, Priya," he said, stressing each word. "Can you believe it?" he asked, placing his hand on my cheek lovingly.

I looked in his eyes. The sincerity they showed. The love they portrayed. I closed my eyes and nodded.

"Naega neo-ege kiseuhaedo dwae?" he whispered hoarsely.

And even though my eyes were closed, I knew what he was asking. I could read it in his tone.

"Can I?" he asked, getting so closer that I felt his nose brushing against my face, his lips mere inches from mine.

Swallowing, with eyes still closed, I shook my head, because he and I could never happen. I know he will burn me, but I didn't want to burn him in the process too. So, I replied, "No, you cannot kiss me CJ! Sorry."

24

An unfinished conversation

It was an awkward drive for a while. I felt his emotions but he didn't react negatively. Instead, he was a perfect gentleman, handling rejection calmly. This is what I liked about CJ, he didn't force me to anything. He asked my permission, I said no, so instead of sulking, making me feel guilty, he simply accepted it and let it slide.

"How far?" I asked after a while. We were driving through breathtaking landscapes, lush greenery stretching as far as the eye could see. Spring had painted the world in delicate hues, fresh green leaves, vibrant blossoms in pinks, yellows, and whites, nature at its finest.

He spoke, and I read on the tablet, "Another hour!"

"How is it that you don't speak English? I read that many people in Seoul do, and considering you're such a prominent personality, shouldn't you? I mean, you interact with people from all over the world, so… shouldn't you know English?" I asked, my curiosity getting the better of me.

He started speaking in Korean, and I glanced down at the tablet to read, "English is, yes, very common language, but it never fascinated me. Until, umm, recently," he grinned sideways at me, and I felt the warmth of a blush creeping up my cheeks.

"So, you only studied Korean?" I asked, deliberately ignoring the heat rushing to my face.

"I studied Mandarin as an alternate language, and German and French… I'm fluent in them. But I also know Spanish and a bit of English, as you know…" he smiled, teasing.

"Wow!" I whispered, genuinely impressed.

"I am planning to learn English and Hindi properly now," he glanced at me before returning his focus to the road, a grin playing on his lips.

"You don't need to learn Hindi," I informed him. "In India, everyone speaks English at work."

"But not at home, isn't it? I noticed during our video calls that your family mostly speaks Hindi," he pointed out.

"Everyone speaks Hindi or their mother tongue at home. It's just… natural," I shrugged.

"So, if I don't know Hindi, how would I form a bond with your children? Wouldn't they always see me as an outsider if they can only speak to me in English?" he asked.

I blinked. He was thinking that far ahead?

"My kids don't speak English that well," I admitted, my voice quieter. "Their English is like yours… very basic."

"Really?" he raised an eyebrow.

"Well, with just my salary, I haven't been able to put them in schools that focus on English. They study in a public school, which is fine, but… it lacks in many facets," I confessed, a tinge of guilt in my voice.

"Not for long," he sighed. "You know, there are quite a few English-speaking schools in Seoul? They offer a holistic education and much more!"

My jaw dropped.

"I… what are you even saying?" I asked, my voice tinged with disbelief.

"The session in these schools normally starts in August or September, so we can plan accordingly!" he continued as if discussing a casual weekend getaway.

"What are you talking about?" I demanded.

"I am talking about you and your family moving to Seoul," he stated, so matter-of-factly that I almost choked. But his tone – oh, his tone – held something undeniably firm, almost commanding.

"Am I reading this right?" I asked, pointing at the tablet, half-hoping I had misunderstood.

"It is always right!" he smirked. "I developed it. You have no idea how much money other companies would offer me if they knew this technology existed, or, for that matter, Mr Choi Man-Young."

I stiffened at the mention of his father but chose to ignore it for now.

"We will circle back to you selling your tech to your bio-dad," I hesitated, "but first, what do you mean by," I paused, reading his words aloud, "I am talking about you and your family moving to Seoul."

He sighed and then spoke, "Why don't we get through today and then decide?"

"What? I mean… *matlab… tum… tumhara dimag kharab hai kya?"* I blurted out in Hindi, my brain struggling to comprehend the audacity of his words.

"No, I don't think I am out of my mind," he replied, his tone entirely too serious.

"You really can understand Hindi?" I gasped.

And he pouted.

"How?" I pressed, narrowing my eyes.

He hesitated for a moment before pulling the car to the side. Then, reaching up, he tweaked his right ear and pulled out something incredibly small.

He pulled out his phone and tapped away at it for a moment before finally looking up at me. "Done. Hair," he said with a smirk as he pointed at my face.

I just stared at the tiny device in his hand… it was minuscule, not even the size of my little fingernail, blinking rapidly. It looked futuristic, almost unreal.

He smiled, reaching out to brush my hair back. My breath fastened at the gentle touch of his fingers on my skin. Slowly, he tucked the little thing onto my right ear and said, "It is a listening device."

I jumped. His voice muffled in my left ear as I still heard him in Korean, but from my right ear, I could hear an automatic voice, clear and crisp, in English.

"Whatever I say, in any language, it will auto-translate to English," he smiled. "When I wear it, the translation setting is Korean, since I understand it best. But for now, I've changed it to English for you."

My jaw dropped.

"You had this, and you never shared it with me?" I demanded, half in awe, half in outrage.

He narrowed his eyes, snatched the tablet, and muttered, "I need to learn English very soon."

"Repeat what you just said?" he asked, and I did.

"Ah! I just have one. It's one of a kind, my design. I will, of course, make more now, but haven't found the time yet."

"This is… incredible," I whispered, still in disbelief.

"It's my lifeline, honestly," he smirked. "No one knows I have it. You have no idea the things I hear from people around me."

"I can imagine," I nodded, carefully reaching up to take it off. But before I could, he grabbed my hand.

"Me," he pointed at himself and removed the device instead. It was almost shocking how much quieter the world felt without it.

He placed it back on his ear with a sigh, then spoke something with a laugh.

I glanced at the tablet, only to see Korean symbols.

"Please change the language here," I huffed, and he chuckled before tweaking a setting on his phone. The tablet refreshed, and English words filled the screen.

"What did you say before?" I asked.

"It felt like I was missing a limb," he repeated, laughing as he started the car again.

"I can imagine. But before we drop this conversation… CJ, I am not moving to Korea. We have just met, we don't even know each other properly. And…" I sighed. "And I cannot ask my family to uproot their lives."

He pressed his lips together at that but didn't argue. Instead, he kept driving.

But I knew, deep down, that this conversation was far from over.

25

Bath, bubbles and towels

It was around seven in the morning when we finally stopped at a hotel. CJ handed the keys to the valet, and we walked in. It was like stepping into a dream. The sheer grandeur of this place could make even the most luxurious five-star hotels feel shy.

He strode confidently to the reception, picked up a key, and led me toward the elevator.

"What are we doing here?" I whispered, feeling a strange unease settle over me. The thought of being alone with him in an elevator, let alone a hotel room, made my pulse quicken. What exactly was he planning?

"We fresh up here," he said with a small smile. "Then we go."

"You booked a room in this extravagant place just to freshen up?" I asked incredulously. "How far is the guesthouse from here?" The unnecessary expense was making me uneasy.

He stared at me, as if I had just asked him if the sky was green. Then he spoke, "Guesthouse have people, they interfere, private time," he gestured between us meaningfully.

A flutter stirred in my chest. Private time? What exactly did he mean by that?

Trying to ignore the strange flutter in my chest, I glanced around at the hotel's stunning interior. Everything screamed opulence.

He unlocked the door to our suite, and within minutes, our bags were delivered.

"Umm…" he hesitated as he tipped the bellboy and dismissed him. Then, looking at the lavishly furnished room, he spoke again. "You get fresh first," he pointed toward the bathroom. "I am back in some time, okay?"

"No… no, you go first," I sighed, already eyeing the incredibly perfect bed longingly. "I just want to rest a bit."

He nodded, motioning toward the bed as if giving me permission to collapse on it. Then, opening his suitcase, he started looking for something.

But I hesitated. The room suddenly felt too small, too intimate. The idea of us being in this space together, even temporarily, made my heart race. He gave me a quizzical look and then sighed.

Muttering something in Korean, he turned away. I hurried over to the table where I had left the tablet and read his words.

"You have nothing to fear from me. If I haven't kissed you without permission, you think I would do anything else?"

A wave of guilt washed over me. He was right. He had never once crossed any boundaries. He was always careful, always respectful.

"I'm not worried about that," I murmured.

He huffed in exasperation, grabbed my shoulders, and literally pushed me onto the bed. I gasped at the suddenness of it. He straightened the tablet in my hands and spoke firmly. "I will take some time in the bathroom. Close your eyes and rest."

Then, pulling the softest, most luxurious blanket over me, he walked away.

When I woke up next, I nearly had a heart attack.

CJ was lying next to me.

Holy hell!

Not under the same blanket, thank God, but still on the same bed. With me.

I bolted upright and almost tumbled right off.

"No trust," he murmured lazily, shifting into a more comfortable position but keeping his eyes closed. Then, in Korean, he muttered something else.

My heart still hammering, I glanced at the tablet, it read, "This girl is absolutely crazy."

Despite myself, I smiled. "I'm not crazy," I muttered under my breath as I hurried into the bathroom.

And then I stopped. Completely stunned.

It was insanely luxurious.

The bathroom was a dream… white marble, gold accents, a mirror the size of a door. And the bathtub.

It wasn't just a bathtub. It was a royal-sized, spa-like masterpiece. Huge enough for two people, with sleek modern designs and a wide shower panel on the side.

I had never taken a bath in a tub before, and the idea of it suddenly felt too tempting.

I peeked back into the room. CJ was still asleep.

Biting my lip, I turned on the taps, watching as the warm water poured in. I grabbed two small bottles labelled 'bubble bath' and dumped them both in, watching with delight as frothy white foam bloomed over the surface.

For such a massive tub, it filled surprisingly fast.

I didn't overthink it. Stripping down, I stepped inside, sighing as the hot water wrapped around me like a comforting embrace.

It was heaven.

I leaned back, my muscles slowly unwinding. How had I gone so many years without experiencing this? And then, as always, my mind betrayed me.

My kids would never experience something like this.

The thought made my chest ache.

I had barely given them any luxuries in life. Could I ever? Maybe if I stayed with CJ, they could have things I had never dreamed of. But was his offer real? Could I trust it?

Wouldn't it be like… taking advantage of him?

And even if we tried, how would it work? We barely knew each other. We didn't speak the same language. He was royalty. And me? I was nothing.

He wanted me, no us, to move to Seoul. What if things didn't work out?

I shuddered at the thought. Could I survive without him in a foreign country?

Could I even survive with him?

A sudden knock made me jump.

"Enjoying?"

My heart froze.

I turned sharply and realized my worst mistake.

The door. I had forgotten to close the damn door.

And CJ was standing right there.

He smirked, leaning against the doorway.

"Nice?" he asked, one brow raised.

The bubbles were thick, forming a soft, frothy blanket over the water, cocooning me in warmth. Only the tops of my bare shoulders peeked through, shimmering under the dim glow of the bathroom lights. A strange unease settled in my chest as I became acutely aware of my nakedness beneath the comforting layer of foam.

I sighed, releasing the tension within me. "Very," I murmured in response to a question I barely remembered.

CJ watched me for a moment, his gaze unreadable. Then, after a pause, he asked, "What thinking?"

I shook my head, closing my eyes, letting the warmth seep into my skin.

But my peace was short-lived. The water shifted, rippling gently around me. My eyes fluttered open just in time to see him submerging into the tub as well, on the opposite side, facing me.

So, I was right. The tub was big enough that I didn't feel his body pressed against mine. But I was hyper-aware of him. His presence. His warmth. His bare shoulders gleaming just above the water.

I swallowed as he closed his eyes, settling into the moment.

"Nice, yes," he murmured, almost to himself.

A sudden wave of nervous energy coursed through me. I wanted to get out, but the towel, my only salvation, was placed behind him, just out of reach.

Before I could figure out my next move, I felt it. A gentle touch. His fingertips grazing up my leg, stopping just at my knee.

"Okay?" he asked, eyes still closed.

I swallowed, but words failed me. Was I okay? Hell no. How could I be okay with him touching me like this?

And yet... I was.

His touch wasn't intrusive or demanding. It was slow, deliberate, almost hesitant… like he was waiting for me to pull away. But I didn't. His fingers traced lazy circles against my skin, featherlight yet leaving a trail of warmth in their wake. A shiver ran through me; not of fear, but of something else. Something deeper. Something I wasn't sure I was ready to name.

I should have pulled away. I should have told him to stop. But instead, I leaned in, just slightly, barely noticeable. But he noticed. His body mirrored mine, shifting closer, and suddenly, I felt his leg brush against my thigh. A spark ignited within me, spreading through my veins like wildfire.

"CJ," I whispered, my voice hoarse with unspoken emotions.

"Hmm?" he hummed lazily, as if he hadn't just set my entire body alight with a single touch.

"I should go," I managed.

His eyes snapped open at my words.

"Go where?" he asked, his voice laced with something I couldn't quite place.

"To get dressed," I mumbled.

A beat of silence passed before he replied. "Okay," his tone was even, but I could sense the shift in the air between us. He withdrew his hand, moving away just enough that the loss of his touch sent an ache through me.

"CJ," I started again, but he ignored me.

"Go," he said after a pause, turning his face away.

He was giving me privacy, but my problem remained – my towel was behind him.

I hesitated, unsure how to phrase my request, but he seemed in no mood to listen. Taking a deep breath, I slowly shifted through the water, dragging as many bubbles with me as possible. I reached for the towel, but it was just beyond my grasp. I needed to move closer.

Biting my lip, I leaned over him, still covering my chest with one arm, stretching as far as I could. Just a little more…

The moment I felt the towel between my fingers, the soapy water betrayed me.

I slipped.

Right on top of him.

A sharp inhale. A swift, steadying grip. And then… warmth.

My bare skin met his, my chest pressed against his solid one, and time itself seemed to halt. His arms tightened around me instinctively, steadying me before I could slip further. My breath hitched as our faces hovered mere inches apart, our eyes locking in silent shock.

"Sorry," I whispered, barely able to form the word. "Towel… I slipped."

His grip on me remained firm, his body tense beneath mine.

I shifted, trying to move away, but the slickness of the water betrayed me once again. I slipped closer instead, and his arm found its way around my back, his touch careful, steady.

"Wait," he murmured, his voice rough, restrained.

And then it hit me.

Here I was, lying on top of him, completely bare, and he hadn't taken advantage of the situation. He hadn't let his hands wander. He hadn't looked at me with anything but patience and concern.

Instead, he took my hand, placing it gently on his shoulder. "Now shift," he instructed, his voice quiet, controlled.

I stared at him, at the solid warmth beneath my fingertips. At the way he was holding himself back.

"Priya," he whispered, his breath warm against my face. "Move, please."

But in that moment, I didn't want to move away. I wanted something else.

And for the first time in my life, I acted on what I truly wanted.

I bent down and kissed him.

26

Happy Birthday!

He stiffened. He didn't kiss me back.

That was not something I had expected. A rush of emotions coursed through me... embarrassment and confusion. He didn't kiss me back! A wave of rejection stormed over me. I have never kissed anyone before, well, I have had many horrible things done to me, but a loving, affectionate, passionate kiss was something new for me. And given how he had kissed me on cheeks, forehead, hand before, I thought... I thought...

I pulled back slightly, my breath uneven, eyes burning with the tears of rejection. I did not even want to look up at him, but I could feel his gaze on me. So, despite myself, with my heart pounding in my chest, I searched his face for an answer, but all I found was restraint, tension, and something dark simmering beneath his stormy gaze.

I shifted, intending to move away, but the soapy water was really not my friend, and I slipped once more. This time, he didn't catch me. I tumbled back into the water, a surprised gasp leaving my lips as I felt something firm, unyielding, press against my waist. Heat flooded my cheeks, my pulse skyrocketing at the realization that he too was turned on and I wasn't the only one struggling to contain whatever was building between us.

So, why didn't he kiss me back? Maybe he saw me almost naked and realized I was so hideous that he didn't want me like that!

"I need a towel," I murmured, barely able to form words, pointing to where it lay behind him. But he didn't move, didn't acknowledge my request. Instead, he was staring at me, his gaze dark, intense.

"Not the best place," he finally rasped, swallowing hard.

I blinked, trying to steady my thoughts. "What?"

"This," his voice was hoarse as he gestured around us. "Not the best place."

"For what?" I whispered as I pulled back further, my voice barely audible over the sound of the water lapping against us.

"For this."

And before I could react, his hand curled around the back of my neck, and suddenly, I was in his lap, my body flush against his. His lips crashed into mine with a hunger that left me breathless, stealing every thought from my mind. He kissed me like he had been holding back for far too long, like he needed this as much as I did.

The kiss deepened, his tongue teasing, tasting, claiming. My hands found his shoulders, gripping them for support as my body melted into his. I barely noticed when I shifted, straddling his waist, until I felt his arms wrap around me, pulling me even closer. The warm water sloshed around us, our bodies half-submerged, but nothing else existed in that moment… only him, only us.

He groaned against my lips, breaking away just enough to let his forehead rest against mine. "We should stop," he breathed, his voice thick with longing.

My chest rose and fell rapidly, my skin flushed and tingling. "You want to stop now?" I asked, my voice shaking with unrestrained desire.

His gaze flickered downward, to where our bodies met... where my bare chest was pressed against his, my hardened peaks grazing his heated skin. His jaw clenched, his fingers flexing on my waist as if he were using every ounce of control he had left.

"God, no," he admitted, his voice strained. "I want you right now. But you..."

I swallowed hard, understanding what he meant. He was holding back for me, stopping because he thought I wasn't ready. But for what? For whom was I saving myself? And was there anything left of me that needed saving?

My fingers slid into his damp hair, tugging slightly until his gaze met mine once more. His pupils were blown wide, his chest rising and falling in sync with mine.

"But me..." I whispered, my lips ghosting over his, my body aching for him.

"Priya," he groaned, his voice full of barely contained restraint.

"Yes?"

"Don't," he whispered, his hands tightened on my hips, his fingers digging into my skin as if he were holding himself back from taking what we both wanted.

"Don't what?" I asked, as I pressed my lips to his throat and he groaned with passion. His entire body jerking with desire.

"I…" he started but I pressed my lips firmly on his. This time he didn't freeze, his lips moved with mine, even hungrily this time.

And I knew what I had to do… I wanted him, no matter the future, no matter the consequences. So, firming my resolve, I moved.

"Happy birthday," I murmured, my lips curving into the faintest of smiles before I shifted, aligning myself against him. A sharp breath hissed through his teeth as he realized what I was doing. His hands gripped me tighter, as if giving me one last chance to change my mind.

But I didn't.

Instead, I let myself sink down, gasping at the exquisite sensation of him filling me completely.

His breath stuttered, his head falling back, his grip on my body turning possessive, reverent.

And in that moment, as our bodies and souls intertwined, nothing else mattered but the way we fit, the way we moved, the way we became one.

27

Silencing the silent questions

That day felt nothing short of magical, a memory I wanted to hold onto forever. We spent it wrapped around each other, lost in soft touches, warm breaths, and the kind of closeness that made the world outside fade away. I didn't even remember when we had moved from the warm water of the bathtub to the bed, where we lay tangled together, our hearts beating in sync, as if we had always belonged this way.

It still amazed me how I had gone from feeling awkward about being alone with him to lying beside him, completely exposed… not just physically but emotionally too. It was as if something inside me had shifted, breaking through all my fears and doubts. But I had no complaints. How could I, when his touch sent shivers down my skin, when his kisses made my heart race, when the way he looked at me made me feel like the most precious thing in the world?

He held me like he was afraid to let go, as if he could keep me in this moment forever. And honestly, I wished he could. Like there was nothing beyond this bed, beyond his arms…

no past, no future, just us. I wanted to freeze time, to soak in the warmth of his body, the safety of his embrace, the way his hands traced every inch of me like he was memorizing something sacred.

But even in all this happiness, a weight pressed down on my heart, a truth I kept shoving deeper inside me. No matter how hard I tried to ignore it, the reality of my past, my present, and my future kept crashing down on me, threatening to break the fragile bubble of peace I had found in his arms. It was always there, lurking in the back of my mind, a silent storm waiting to shatter everything. And yet, for now, I pushed it away… desperate to hold onto this moment, even if I knew it couldn't last forever. But I knew he could sense it. He always could. His touch, no matter how gentle, searched for the words I wasn't ready to say. His eyes, even filled with love, tried to see past the walls I have built. And every time I felt his silent questions, I silenced him instead by kissing him, holding him, pulling him closer, giving him every distraction I could.

But I knew this couldn't last. The safety of this room would disappear the moment we stepped outside. Sooner or later, I would have to face reality. Sooner or later, I would have to tell him everything, when I would have to bare my soul to him, just as I had bared my body. And when that moment came, I could only hope he would still hold me the same way… with the same love, the same warmth, the same unshakable certainty.

We had ordered lunch in the room, but by 7:30 PM, he had taken my hand and led me downstairs for dinner. The hotel was extravagant, the kind of place where everything gleamed: chandeliers dripped from the ceiling, the floors shone like glass, and the air smelled of money. I felt small in my plain, unbranded clothes, like I didn't belong. But he didn't see it that way. He wrapped his arm around my waist, pulling me close, guiding me through the grand space like I was the most precious thing in the world. Like I belonged right there, beside him.

We didn't speak much. We hadn't talked much during the day either. Our bodies had done all the talking. And even now, as we sat side by side in the dimly lit restaurant, our legs brushing, his fingers playing lazily with mine, his touch was saying everything that words couldn't.

"So, how is your birthday going?" I asked, just to break the quiet silence between us. Though I already knew the answer.

He cocked his eyebrow at this. "You have to ask?" he whispered. His hand moved, slipping beneath the heavy tablecloth, tracing slow circles on my thigh. My breath caught, my body betraying me. Every brush of his fingers sent a jolt of electricity through me, a fire that pooled low in my stomach. I clenched my thighs together, trying to stay composed, but he noticed. Of course, he noticed. He always did.

I saw it in the way his jaw tensed, in the way he shifted slightly, his eyes flickering with something dark and heated.

"So, a good birthday?" I swallowed hard and asked, not for him, but to stop myself from moaning right then and there.

"Can get better," he smirked, reading my expressions.

"How?" I asked, intrigued, but still in a daze, but he didn't reply. He just shook his head and continued to eat.

I also ate quietly, as much as I could with his hands firmly gripping my upper thigh.

"I want more," he murmured as he finished the last bite of his food.

I reached for the menu, thinking he meant dessert, but before I could, he caught my hand. His grip was firm, his thumb brushing over my palm in a way that made my breath stutter.

"I want more," he repeated, his voice lower this time, his gaze lingering on my lips.

I licked my lips, my body rooted to the spot. The tension between us was thick, crackling like a live wire, so intense that I was surprised the whole restaurant hadn't turned to watch us, that the air around us wasn't on fire.

"Back to the room?" he asked, his voice rough as he swallowed hard.

I nodded, unable to speak, my entire body already humming in anticipation.

He muttered something in Korean under his breath, but as usual, I didn't understand. I fumbled for the tablet, and he repeated. The tablet translated flawlessly, as usual.

"We need to go to the chemist first," the screen read.

Confused, I frowned. "Are you not feeling well?" I asked, reaching out to place my palm on his forehead.

He let out a low chuckle, catching my hand and pressing a heavy kiss to my knuckles before leaning in close, his breath warm against my ear.

"I forgot condoms," he whispered in my ear, nibbling at it gently, his voice husky, sending shivers down my spine.

My face heated instantly. "Too late now, isn't it?" I murmured, barely able to hold his gaze, the nearness of him making my head spin.

He hummed, his lips brushing along my throat, making my pulse race. "And a pill for you," he added, his mouth moving to my neck, sucking lightly.

"I don't need it," I breathed, pulling back just enough to meet his eyes.

He blinked, surprised, his grip on my hand tightening slightly.

"Let's go," I said quickly, smiling as I tried to push away the weight of reality threatening to creep in. I didn't want to ruin this moment. I didn't want to ruin *us*. Not tonight.

He blinked again, as if trying to figure me out.

"Let's go," I repeated, this time letting my own hand slide up his thigh, slowly, teasingly. "I want more too."

His body tensed instantly beneath my touch, his breath faltering for a moment. He was about to ask questions, I could see it in his eyes, but the second my hand reached the top of his thigh, any words he had died in his throat.

He swallowed hard, muttered something quickly in Korean, then grabbed my hand and pulled me up, leading me out of the restaurant. Heads turned as we walked past, people watching, maybe sensing the fire burning between us, but I didn't care. My eyes were fixed on the screen of the tablet he held in his free hand.

It read: 'I want answers, but right now, I want you more. So, I'll have you first, and then I'll have my answers.'

And I wasn't sure whether to be thrilled or terrified.

28

Not today!

We left the hotel the next morning… reluctantly. He was in no hurry to go, wanting nothing more than to stay tangled in bed with me for a little longer. But his phone, which had been blissfully silent the entire day before, was now buzzing incessantly with calls and messages.

He let out a frustrated growl as he finally answered a relentless caller, his tone clipped and impatient. With a heavy sigh, he got dressed, but not before we stole one last shower together… one last moment of passion, one last chance to drown in each other before stepping back into reality.

As he drove us back, his fingers intertwined with mine, he asked, almost casually, "So, why no pill?"

It was just past seven in the morning, and I knew we were already too late for work. The prototype was due in a few weeks, and there was still so much left to be done. And after that, I would go back to India… *forever.*

I didn't respond.

Sensing my silence, he gently squeezed my fingers.

"Please," I whispered, my voice barely holding together as emotion tightened my throat.

He glanced at me, his brows furrowing in concern. "Why no pill?" he asked again, softer this time.

"I'm happy, CJ," I whispered, though in that moment, I wasn't. My heart felt impossibly heavy, as if it might burst from the sheer weight of everything I was holding inside.

He slowed the car to a stop on the side of the road, turning to me fully. His warm palm cupped my cheek, his thumb brushing lightly against my skin. "What's wrong?"

I exhaled shakily, trying to keep the storm of emotions from breaking free, but it was no use. "I'm happy for the first time since my mother died, CJ. *I'm happy.* Please…" My voice cracked, and despite my best efforts, tears spilled down my cheeks.

His expression shifted… concern, confusion, something close to fear flashing across his face. "Your mother?" he asked seriously.

I nodded, sniffing, my hands trembling in my lap.

"When she die?" he asked, and I knew he meant to say *when did she die?*

"She died when I was eight." The words barely left my lips before the tears started falling in earnest, an unstoppable flood.

His frown deepened. "And you not happy since?" His voice was laced with disbelief, as if he couldn't comprehend the depth of my pain.

I shook my head. "Please don't ask me… not today. Let me be happy today, please." And without thinking, I grabbed his hand, clutching it tightly, and burying my face in his palm, I sobbed.

He didn't say anything. He didn't press. He just let me cry, his fingers threading through my hair as his other hand rested on my back.

When my sobs finally quieted, when I had pulled myself together, he wordlessly reached for a bottle of water, handing it to me along with some wet wipes to clean my face. Then, without another word, he started driving again.

The rest of the ride was silent, though I caught him stealing glances at me every now and then… worried, thoughtful. And deep down, a gnawing fear took root in my chest. Had I scared him? Had I let him see too much? Was this the moment he realized I was too broken, too much for him to handle?

When we pulled into the office parking lot, he cut the engine but didn't move right away. Instead, he turned to me, his expression unreadable. Then, with a quiet sigh, he leaned in and pressed his lips gently to my forehead.

"Don't worry. I won't ask," he murmured against my skin.

But before he could pull away, I cupped his face and kissed him, firm, deep, desperate. "I will tell you," I whispered against his lips. "I owe you that. Just… not today."

His gaze searched mine, his fingers tightening around my waist as he repeated, "Not today."

Then, he kissed me back.

29

Confessions and more

Alex was delighted to see me back. The moment he spotted me, he pulled me into a tight hug, grinning from ear to ear as we walked to the floor together. CJ, however, wasn't as amused. He frowned at Alex's open display of affection before wordlessly striding into his cabin.

"So, tell me everything. What kept you back in India?" Alex demanded, dragging me into a long conversation that stretched through the next few hours as we worked side by side.

As usual, CJ disappeared around five, and by seven, Chirag was the one walking me back to the guesthouse. To my surprise, he stayed for dinner. It wasn't like him… he usually dropped me off and left, but tonight, he lingered, steering the conversation towards my home, my family… and CJ.

When we had finished eating, he asked, "Should we go for a walk?"

I nodded, still taken aback by his unusual company.

We had barely stepped out, just beyond the earshot of Ha-Yoon, the nosy caretaker of the guesthouse, when Chirag spoke. "Are you involved with Mr Choi?" he asked, almost too casually.

I stopped mid-step, startled. "What? No!"

His eyes studied my face, unreadable. So, I added, "Why are you asking?"

"Well…" he hesitated. "The word is, he left Seoul right after you did. Then, he diverted his flight to India before coming back. And both of you were missing yesterday," his lips twisted into a knowing grimace.

I felt my face heat up. I couldn't deny what he was implying, but I still shrugged it off. "He's Mr Choi, Chirag," I sighed. "And I… I am a beggar in comparison."

"So, you're *not* involved with him?" he pressed.

I let out a short laugh, shaking my head. "Not even if I wanted to be. Do you really see someone like him with someone like me? Do we even have a future?"

Chirag didn't answer, he just stared, so I said what he had told me weeks ago. I raised my hand as high as I could and said, "He is *there*…" then instead of pointing somewhere just above ground, I tapped my foot against the ground with deliberate force highlighting the stark difference, "…and I am *here*. There is no horizon where we could ever be together."

His expression tightened, "Do you *want* to be with him?"

I exhaled, a small smile forming on my lips. "He is nice, yes. And very handsome," I chuckled softly. "I like him."

Chirag cursed under his breath.

"Why do you even ask?" I teased. "Did you place a bet or something?"

He looked startled but quickly recovered. "When you were gone… I realized something," he muttered.

"What did you realize, Chirag?" I asked simply.

He exhaled sharply, "I like you."

Shock rippled through me at his words. What! And why? Suddenly, why were these guys throwing attention at me? Ashok, CJ, and now Chirag? I was a nobody, an invisible girl, and yet!

"I am serious," he added.

"Don't," I whispered, shaking my head.

"But I…" he started but I raised my hand and stopped him.

"Chirag, I am sorry, you are my friend, a *friend,"* I stressed. "Please…"

A stunned silence stretched between us before I finally repeated, "I'm sorry, Chirag. And I think you are mistaken. You told me once I am the only Indian girl you have met in the past three years. You are mistaking our friendly bond for something else…"

"You cannot determine how I feel," he spoke hotly.

I sighed. "Fine! But I don't like you like that," I replied sadly.

His face twisted in frustration. "But you like *him*," he said bitterly. "Of course, with him around all the time, how could you not?"

I sighed again, my shoulders sagging. "I don't *like* anyone like that, Chirag, especially him."

"I don't believe you," he hissed.

And I repeated, "He is there, Chirag…" I pointed at the sky. "And I am there, literally in the dirt!" and I stomped my feet on the ground. "In no world, he and I belong."

"But we can belong," Chirag insisted.

"No, I don't…" I started but his gaze suddenly shifted, locking onto something behind me.

"If you both are so different," he muttered darkly, "then what is he doing here at this hour?"

A chill ran down my spine as I turned and saw CJ.

He stood beside his car, no more than ten steps away, watching us, maybe even listening to us.

Chirag exhaled sharply, "You could've told me the truth," he murmured. "Before I shared my feelings with you."

I swallowed, "He always takes me back to the office. It's not safe here at night. We work together."

Chirag lifted a sceptical eyebrow, "Yeah, right!"

CJ walked over; his expression unreadable.

"Mr Choi," Chirag greeted begrudgingly, bowing slightly.

CJ gave him a slow, lazy nod.

Then, looking at me, CJ said, "Come," his voice was firm, unquestionable. "Office. And then… more."

My eyes widened. Did he mean…? *Where? How…?*

He turned to Chirag and spoke something in Korean, to which Chirag responded equally curtly.

Then, with a dry chuckle, Chirag muttered in Hindi, *"Kuch bhi bol lo, sab dikhta hai."* (Translation: You can say whatever you want, but I can see everything.)

And with that, he walked away.

I stood frozen, watching my only friend in this foreign country disappear into the night.

CJ's voice cut through my thoughts. "We'll deal with that," he nodded in Chirag's direction, "later."

"Yeah, let's go to work," I spoke sadly, my eyes still lingering where Chirag had disappeared.

CJ tapped his foot impatiently, "Do you really think you belong there?"

I blinked, confused. He had heard. Damn it!

"Yeah… I do," I replied, voice soft.

He narrowed his eyes at me. "And you believe we can't be together?" he asked, glancing back at his tablet.

"You tell me. Do we?" I shot back, trying to keep my voice even but feeling the crack underneath.

He tilted his head, curious but silent.

And while I had spoken similar things before, how could I not re-iterate them when I knew who he truly was. I blabbed, "I mean, look at us. I'm a beggar, literally. A girl with no background, no money, no home. Nothing. And you… you're a billionaire."

He pursed his lips but didn't say a word. That silence… it burned.

Frustrated, I reached out and placed my hand on his.

"Look at this," I said, forcing him to meet my gaze. He stared down at our hands.

"You're perfect," I whispered, my voice trembling. "Just… too damn perfect. And I'm…"

Tears welled in my eyes. I tried to hold them back, but the contrast between us was too glaring.

"You and I, CJ… ours is a love that cannot last."

He exhaled deeply and glanced around. The guesthouse was in clear view. I knew Ha-yoon was probably spying again.

"Come," CJ said softly.

But I shook my head.

"I can't say what I need to without touching you. And I don't want Ha-yoon snapping more photos," CJ sighed, reading from his tablet. "So… shall we?" he asked, unlocking his car.

I sniffed and followed him in silence.

He drove quietly, the tension thick, until we reached the office parking lot. He parked, checked that we were alone, then finally turned to face me.

"Here," he shoved the tablet into my lap.

"What's wrong with you?" he snapped.

I looked up, startled at his tone and words.

"No, seriously," he said, his voice rising. "Why do you keep on saying all these things about yourself? Do you have *no* self-worth?"

I just stared, stunned into silence.

"You really believe you're in the dirt and I'm in the sky? Are you insane?" he almost shouted and I flinched.

"You said you have no background, no money, what else?" he spat, trying to recall. "Why do you think so little of yourself?"

As a tear trickled down my cheek, his voice softened just a bit. "You're a genius. You're smart, bold, driven. Do you not see how special you are?" he asked.

I let out a dry laugh. Me? Special?

"You said it yourself… you've been raising three kids on a single salary. You think that's easy? You're selfless. You're strong. You're extraordinary. And yet, you talk like you're worthless."

"You don't know anything," I whispered.

"Then tell me," he said, eyes blazing. "Tell me everything, and then I'll tell you how wrong you are."

"CJ, you and I…" I began, but he grabbed my hand and placed it on his again.

"This contrast," he pointed between our hands. "You think my hands are perfect?"

"They are," I said softly, unable to look away from his flawless skin.

"Because all I've ever done is use them on a laptop," he said bitterly, "But your hands?"

He looked down at mine and grabbed them protectively, "Your hands are lined with your life. With hard work.

Struggle. Survival. They tell stories of grit, of strength. You rose from nothing and built something."

I couldn't speak. His words echoed in my chest like a steady drumbeat, shaking something loose inside me.

"How can you dismiss your own life's work like this?" he asked, his tone sad.

I didn't know what to say, so I just stayed quiet.

"And why can't we last?" he asked, more intensely now.

I kept staring at the words on the tablet, unable to meet his eyes. So he reached out, gently took my chin, and tilted my face toward him.

"You think you can just leave… but you should know, I will stay here, holding onto memories that will keep me breaking me over and over again…"

My eyes welled up at these words. Did he really mean them? Were his feelings really so deep?

"Why can't we last, Priya?" he repeated, this time softer.

"Because we come from different worlds," I whispered and he laughed.

"This…" he waved around, still holding my face "…with you, this world is mine. But where is *your* world?"

"With you?" I asked, stunned by the realization.

And he smiled.

"And this feels like home," he said, and then leaned in and kissed me, slow, firm, full of love and all the passion he had been holding back.

And in that moment, I did feel it.

Home.

"How about you?" he asked, pulling back.

I nodded, unable to speak, the storm of emotions crashing inside me.

"So do you still think we don't belong together?" he asked.

I just shook my head solemnly.

"Finally," he exhaled, a teasing smile playing on his lips as he kissed me again, "shall we go home now? Because I want to show you how I feel and how we can be together. And Priya..." he paused as he swallowed, "I *really* do want more."

30
A new place

CJ drove us through the city, his hand resting possessively on my thigh, fingers tracing idle circles that sent small, delicious shivers up my spine. The car glided to a stop in front of a towering apartment building, sleek and modern, with an air of exclusivity that left no doubt about the kind of people who lived here.

Security was tight: gated entrance, high-end surveillance, a doorman who nodded at CJ as if he were royalty. I followed him inside, still breathless from our earlier conversation, my body humming with residual feelings.

The apartment was stunning. High ceilings, floor-to-ceiling windows offering a breathtaking view of the city skyline, and furniture so elegant it looked untouched. But my attention was quickly drawn to something else… my bag, sitting neatly in the living room.

I frowned realizing I left my stuff in his car that morning. “My things...”

Before I could finish, CJ turned me around, his grip firm, his lips claiming mine in a kiss so deep it stole the breath right out of me. I barely registered the way he lifted me into his arms, carrying me effortlessly toward the plush sofa. His body pressed against mine as he laid me down, his mouth tracing a slow, torturous path along my throat.

"Where are we?" I murmured between ragged breaths.

"Not now," he growled, tugging at my shirt, eyes dark with desire.

And I let him.

Hours later, or so it felt, when the fever had finally subsided, when our bodies lay tangled and spent on the now thoroughly ruined sofa, he exhaled a satisfied groan.

"Still not enough," he murmured against my skin, his voice husky with want. "Always more."

Next when I found my senses, I was no longer in the living room. Instead, I was wrapped in his arms, in a bed… large, luxurious, and unfamiliar. The sheets were soft against my skin, but CJ's warmth was softer.

I blinked up at him, my fingers tracing lazy patterns on his bare chest. "Where are we?"

His lips curved into a slow, knowing smile, but he didn't answer.

I glanced around the room. It was beautifully furnished, but impersonal. No photos, no signs of someone actually living here.

"This isn't your home," I mused, lifting my head. "It's too bare."

"Empty?" he asked, brushing my hair from my face. "It has everything."

I chuckled. "I mean, it feels cold. No personal touches."

His smirk widened, "Umm…" he thought for a moment and then said, "rented. Month."

I propped myself up on one elbow, my brows knitting together. "You rented this apartment for a month?" I asked.

He nodded.

"Umm, isn't moving in together kind of a big decision?" I asked hesitantly.

"Do you… a… want… not…" he asked suddenly.

Oh, how could I tell him that I didn't mind anything regarding him…

"I have seen in a lot of TV shows that moving in is kind of big deal," I replied.

"Is it… a… for you?" he asked again.

"I feel we should do what makes us happy," I smiled.

"Do I make you… a… happy?" he asked, consciously.

I smiled, no… I blushed… hard. How could I tell him how happy he made me…

"So…" he whispered, trailing his finger across my face.

"Are you sure you want to live with me?" I asked.

"No doubt…" he laughed heartily but his eyes held something darker… a deeper desire.

"Why do you want to move-in with me?" I whispered as I asked stared into his darkening gaze.

"Because…" he moved on top of me again, his body pressing perfectly into mine, his arousal unmistakable as he nipped at my collarbone, "I want so much more."

At some point, exhaustion won over desire, and sleep claimed me. When I stirred again, the room was bathed in the soft hues of dawn, the city stretching endlessly beyond the glass walls. CJ was still beside me, but awake… his laptop balanced on his thighs, his fingers flying over the keyboard.

I stretched, muscles aching in ways that made me blush. He glanced at me, his gaze sliding down my body, making no effort to hide his appreciation. Only then did I realize that the sheets had slipped down, leaving me entirely exposed to him.

Heat flushed up my neck, and I instinctively pulled the covers over myself.

His expression darkened. He muttered something in Korean, and then read it from his laptop in English, "You were more generous earlier."

I bit my lip, suppressing a smile, "What are you working on?"

"Prototype," he murmured, typing something, but his eyes kept drifting back to me. "Hard to focus."

I smirked and asked, "Is the internet secure here?"

He nodded absently, watching as I sat up, my back now exposed to him. Excited I turned towards my bag only to remember that my work laptop was locked in office.

"Yes," he smiled as he picked up another laptop from side table and handed it to me. "Already connected you to secure wi-fi."

I beamed as I took the laptop, but he held on to it.

"Now, you don't work nights in the office," he whispered softly.

I chuckled, "My butt will be so thankful."

He raised an eyebrow at that, as if considering something wicked, something unspoken. And I wondered what his translating device must have spoken in his ears.

His grip on the laptop loosened, but before I could fully take it, he moved. In one fluid motion, he shoved both laptops aside and flipped me onto my back, pinning me beneath him.

His voice was thick with desire as he whispered, “First, make my ass happy.”

And then, he devoured me all over again.

31

Dressed, undressed!

A new rhythm soon settled between us, one that spoke of quiet understanding and stolen moments. Before, both CJ and I used to be in the office before eight, but now, our mornings stretched lazily, filled with slow kisses and whispered confessions against bare skin. We arrived together at ten, left together just after seven. Our synchronized arrivals and departures did not go unnoticed, but I didn't care. Some feelings feel right in your heart, even when you know they're meant to end in heartbreak…

Also, I had less than a month to cherish his company, and then I would go… forever. If people wanted to talk, let them. For the first time, any gossip about me revolved around something that brought me happiness rather than misery.

I no longer lived in the guesthouse. This apartment with CJ was now my home in Seoul. It had everything, bed and all furniture of right height, my clothes and all the essentials a girl could need to survive.

CJ was the perfect roommate. He took care of everything even without me asking for it. He had even arranged for a private chef and housekeeper, ensuring that each evening we returned to a spotless home and a warm, delicious meal waiting for us on the dining table.

The first night, we decided to shower before dinner. But showering together was never a quick affair. His touch was a slow burn, his lips mapping every inch of my skin, making the water cascading over us feel almost redundant. We never made it to dinner that night, only to bed, where hunger of a different kind took precedence. The next day, laughing at our lack of self-restraint, we agreed to eat first, talk for a while, and then indulge in our more nefarious activities.

On the morning of the third day in this house, I woke up with a thin wrapped package where CJ should have been. I could hear him speaking to someone outside. Smiling, I opened it, only to find our picture inside a beautiful frame. It was the same picture Ha-yoon had taken of CJ and I, outside guesthouse.

A warm feeling of love and affection cushioned my heart as I caressed his beautiful face in it. I felt my fingers touch something, turning it over, I saw a small note stuck behind the frame with words 'Now home not empty!'

Wrapping the sheets around my body, I quickly hopped in the bathroom to freshen up. And then, still wrapped in sheets I stepped out of the room, to thank CJ properly for his such considerate gift.

Before CJ, I thought I had long since forgotten what it meant to feel this way… to be desired, to be cherished, to be loved without restraint. But now, with him, I found myself constantly craving more. His touch, his care, his unwavering attention… it was intoxicating. The only time I found myself away from him was when he was absorbed in his other ZenTel responsibilities, or when I spoke to my family, which I ensured I did just as often as before.

Then, the weekend arrived. And I dared to hope that we would spend every second of it wrapped up in each other.

But when I woke up, the warmth of him was gone.

I reached for him instinctively, fingers brushing against the empty sheets. Blinking the sleep from my eyes, I sat up, wrapping the sheets around me, and listened. His voice, low and clipped, filtered through the apartment.

Pulling on the crumpled clothes from the night before, I dressed quietly and found him standing by the window, deep in conversation, his expression hard, irritated. I waited, unwilling to interrupt. Instead, I took the time to freshen up, and when I stepped into the shower, the sound of his voice had vanished.

The warm water cascaded down my skin, rinsing away the last remnants of sleep. I reached for my shampoo, lathering the strands between my fingers. And then, I felt his eyes on me.

He didn't say a word, he was standing in the door, staring at me.

"Who was it?" I asked casually, not facing him.

"Choi Man-Young," he replied disgruntled.

I wanted to say something, but the angry snap in his tone was enough for me to not dwell on to the conversation. So, I did the next best thing. I distracted him.

"You are already bored?" I turned to face him, teasingly, my bare body now fully exposed to his gaze. Slowly, I raised my hands to rinse my hair, the movement accentuating every curve, every line, just for him.

"Of what?" he asked as he sucked in a huge breath, his expressions dark, his eyes trailed over my body.

"Bathing with me?" I chuckled, as I turned my back to him again.

But he was quiet. Too quiet... I had hoped to feel his hands on me, but instead, he was gone, I thought.

Sighing, I turned and my breath hitched. Because, he was not gone. Instead, I found him on his knees, water soaking through his shirt, darkening the fabric as he looked up at me with something almost reverent in his eyes.

His gaze darkened even more, lips parting slightly as he exhaled. "Bored of what?" he asked again but his sound faded as he reached out, trailing his fingers up the back of my thigh.

His eyes never left mine.

I swallowed as I realized just where his face was. I tried to pull back, but his nails dug in my hips, stopping me.

"Bored of you?" he repeated with a groan, and slowly, deliberately, he leaned forward, his breath warm against my skin. My heart thundered in my chest as realization dawned.

"Never," he whispered.

And then, without warning, he pressed his face in places that not just stole my breath but also made the world blur around me.

When we finally dressed and stepped out for breakfast, I noticed another door left slightly ajar. My curiosity piqued because in the days I have lived here, the other two rooms of the apartment have remained closed and well, empty! So, I walked toward it, only to be met with an overwhelming sight, i.e. of racks upon racks of clothing in every imaginable colour, style, and fabric. Shelves lined with accessories, shoes arranged neatly in rows, and an entire wall dedicated to evening gowns.

"What?" The shock in my voice was evident as I stepped into the room, running my fingers across the delicate fabrics.

CJ stood behind me, watching my reaction with amusement. Without saying a word, he handed me the tablet, and as I read the translation, he began speaking in Korean.

"Remember that party?" he asked.

I nodded slowly, my gaze still sweeping across the extravagant collection before me.

"Mother is hosting it tonight," he continued, sighing slightly as if bracing himself for my reaction.

"Alright," I responded cautiously, drawing out the word.

"We have to go," he added, the weight of his words settling in the air between us.

"We?" I turned to him, my surprise evident.

"Not going alone," he chuckled. "Not bored enough, you know," his laughter was easy, but the glint in his eyes was unreadable.

I turned back to the endless racks of dresses, "So, I wear one of these?"

"Or something you already have," he said with a shrug. "I just wanted you to have options. You should feel comfortable. Wear whatever you want… anything…" he stressed the last word with deliberate slowness.

I narrowed my eyes at him and pointed at an extremely lacy, barely-there piece of lingerie. "Anything?"

He smirked, stepping closer, his voice dropping to a husky whisper, "This... and something more."

I rolled my eyes, but before I could tease him further, his next words caught me off guard.

"My mother wants to meet you."

My heart sank.

"What? Why?" I turned to him fully now, scanning his face for any sign of a joke.

"Because I told her that I like someone," he shrugged as he spoke in rapid Korean. I read what he said on tablet and goosebumps erupted all over my body.

"But she doesn't even like me," I whispered.

"Actually," he corrected, "she was the one who asked for you."

My head snapped in his direction, and my chest tightened. "But she has issues with my legal age!"

CJ let out a laugh, an actual deep chuckle, before arching an eyebrow at me. "Legal age? Why? Your actual age is different?"

His words, translated on the screen, silenced me. He studied my face for a moment before adding, "Is this part of the 'not now' conversation?"

I nodded.

He nodded too, letting the subject drop, but I could feel his curiosity simmering beneath the surface.

The day unfolded differently than I had imagined. Instead of spending the morning tangled in his arms, he was busy with calls, his attention pulled in every direction. And me? I didn't work that Saturday. Instead, I spent the day trying on dress after dress, admiring my reflection, and second-guessing every choice.

He had given me the freedom to wear anything I wanted, but how could I possibly choose something from my own wardrobe after seeing what he had brought in? And I had to consider his reputation as well!

While I tried on endless dresses, pairing them with matching accessories, a sudden realization struck me. Was Choi Man-Young calling him to ask that I not be brought along? He knew about me, CJ had told me that Choi Man-Young had asked him to stay away from me, a request CJ had outright refused. But did he really ask him not to bring me because… because I wasn't of his standard?

I wanted to ask, but I worried it would upset him further. I peeked outside; he was frowning at his screen, so I decided not to dwell on it. Instead, I resolved to prove to Choi Man-Young how wrong he was. If CJ had chosen me to accompany him, then I would prove that his choice was right!

After much deliberation, I settled on a sleek black dress with delicate, thin straps and a side slit that kissed my thigh just right. It hugged my body in all the right places, making me feel confident and undeniably sensual. I was pleasantly surprised to notice that the little flab on my tummy was almost gone too. I guess regular cycling, walking, and now, all that physical exertion with CJ, had paid off. Blushing at the realization, I paired the dress with elegant heels and minimal jewellery, letting the dress do all the talking.

By the time evening arrived, I took my time getting ready, making sure every detail was perfect. He had told me we needed to leave by 6:30 PM, so by 6, I was standing in front of the full-length mirror, admiring the final look.

Everything was in place, except for one thing: the zipper at the back.

Stepping out of the room, I found him seated on the couch, immersed in his laptop. He didn't even notice me at first. But when his eyes finally lifted, they flickered over my body in a slow, deliberate scan, darkening slightly as they took in how the dress moulded to my curves.

"Help me?" I asked, turning my back to him.

He set his laptop aside, stood up, and approached me. The warmth of his hands ghosted over my skin before gripping the zipper, pulling it up with agonizing slowness. His fingers lingered just a moment longer than necessary, grazing the nape of my neck and sending a shiver down my spine.

I turned to face him, "How do I look?"

He didn't answer immediately. His gaze was heavy, unreadable… but something simmered beneath it. Something possessive. Something dangerous.

"CJ," I whispered, a thought occurring to me as I turned around again, trying to gather the confidence to ask what I wanted.

"Hmm?" he asked, his lips brushing the back of my neck, sending electric currents coursing through me.

"Can I ask you something? If you won't get mad?" I asked, trying very hard not to lose focus.

"Anything," he murmured, his hands firm around my waist, silently demanding what he wanted.

"Are you a sex addict?" I asked suddenly.

His hands froze. His kisses paused. He just stood still.

I quickly turned to face him and continued, "Sorry, and I don't mind it, but… are you?"

He straightened and tilted his head thoughtfully.

"Not think it," he replied, which I took to mean, 'I don't think so.'

"Okay," I nodded, biting my lip.

Then he said something in Korean. I bent down to pick up his tablet. "Repeat, please," I requested.

He did.

I read the translation on the tablet: "No, I'm not a sex addict. Why do you ask?"

"It just came to me, so I asked," I shrugged.

What I didn't tell him was that a part of my brain, the stupid, insecure part, was wondering that if he liked sex this much, who had he been having it with before me? And with whom would he continue once I was gone?

"Really?" he asked, raising an eyebrow. "Well, I like sex. I am not addicted. Though… with you, I just cannot stop."

I blushed hard at that.

"You mind it?" he asked, his English adorably broken but his meaning clear.

"Me?" My eyes widened, "I don't mind. Instead…" I bit my lip, unsure of how to explain what his touch did to me.

"Instead?" he nudged.

"Nothing," I said, closing my eyes with a soft groan.

"Tell me," he urged, his expression so open and sincere, I had to.

"Instead, I love that you want me like that. With you loving me, touching me like that… makes me feel alive, free… loved… protected…" I whispered.

"So, you no mind?" he asked again.

"Never," I said softly, unsure how else to respond.

"Then… let me make you freer," he said with a wicked grin.

"The party?" I reminded him. "It took me so much time to get ready."

"How much time?" he asked, his fingers trailing lightly along my back.

I laughed, "Three hours!"

"Makeup?" he asked, tilting his head.

"That took the longest," I admitted. "I'm not used to doing so much."

He nodded thoughtfully.

"Hair?"

"Not long. I do this style often."

"Good," he murmured, stepping behind me again.

And before I could react, his hand reached for the zipper once more. This time pulling it down instead of up.

My breath hitched.

"Remind me not to touch your face then," he whispered.

And with a swift, deliberate motion, he peeled the dress from my body, undoing every careful effort I had made to get ready.

The party would have to wait.

32

Everyone has a price

We drove for an hour. We had to leave at 6:30 PM but we left at 7:45, which was mainly because his mother was calling him non-stop!

"Why is it everything so far away here?" I mused as we drove.

He chuckled and then said, "Yes, far from all," he laughed.

"Do you mean that you have chosen our apartment away from prying eyes, a bit far away, deliberately?" I asked.

He stared at me for a moment, then smiled and nodded.

"You understand me, despite my Korean," he chuckled.

And I remembered 'language of love' conversation. Was I really falling in love with him? Or had I already fallen?

"Yes, I think I do, most of the times," I smiled as I realized he was waiting for an answer.

When we arrived at the destination, my jaw dropped. I wonder when I will stop getting shocked by his opulence. It was a house, no, it was paradise. Set against the backdrop of mountains, covered in lush greenery, it was so beautiful. The house was a high-class Korean *hanok*, blending traditional architecture with modern luxury. Its curved tiled roof, with intricately carved wooden eaves, stood tall against the serene landscape. The wooden beams, polished to perfection, gleamed under the soft sunlight. Wide sliding doors made of delicate *hanji* paper allowed natural light to pour in, offering a seamless view of the vibrant garden outside. The courtyard, paved with smooth stones, was adorned with bonsai trees and a tranquil koi pond. Every corner exuded elegance, from the ornate lanterns hanging by the entrance to the intricate latticework on the windows. It wasn't just a house… it was a masterpiece, a harmonious blend of tradition and sophistication.

"This is your house?" I asked, astonished. Never in my life had I set foot in such a luxurious place. The sheer magnificence of it was overwhelming.

"Yes," CJ replied with a smile, his fingers wrapping around mine as he gently tugged me forward. "Come."

"I mean…" I hesitated, my eyes sweeping across the grand façade. It was just too much… too lavish, too elegant, too surreal. "This is your home? Why do you live in that apartment then?" Because while the apartment was grand, it was a mere shack in comparison to this house.

"This," he pointed at the house, "Not my home, my mother's home, and that *apateu*," he corrected as he grabbed my waist smugly, his smile deepening as two people rushed out to greet him.

"*Apateu* means apartment, right?" I asked and he nodded, grinning still, completely ignoring the two people now waiting for him.

"What about that *apateu?*" I asked, curious.

"My home, with you," he murmured with such loving sincerity that I was speechless. He pecked my lips softly and then released me. He greeted the two men, introduced me in rapid Korean, which I didn't understand, whatsoever, and then dragged me inside.

But as we walked, I felt a warmth spread in my chest. With him was my home… and then I halted mid-step, shocked at my own thoughts. His home was with me! But where was my home? Back in India, with my children… *Not with him!*

"Come," he urged, not noticing my inner turmoil, and leading me into a grand living room where the air buzzed with lively chatter. The moment we stepped in, the atmosphere shifted. A chorus of greetings and cheers erupted as everyone raised their glasses to him. My gaze swept across the room, there were at least fifty impeccably dressed guests, all eyes fixed on him… and me.

Men regarded me with interest, while the women? Pure jealousy and thinly veiled disdain radiated from their faces. Before I could fully register the scrutiny, the crowd swallowed him up, a sea of voices in rapid Korean drowning my thoughts. I attempted to step aside, but the moment I moved, he tightened his grip on my waist, pulling me close, as if unwilling to let me slip away.

From the periphery, I spotted Chirag and Alex. Unlike the others, they remained on the sidelines, watching with expressions of pure incredulity.

CJ spoke, engaging with the crowd, until a slightly older woman appeared at his side. The effect was instant, everyone melted away, parting like the sea.

CJ guided me to a quiet corner as the woman fussed over him, her voice quick and affectionate. It was clear, this was his mother.

He responded to her, then, with a swift motion, removed the listening device from his ear and placed it gently on mine.

A jolt of surprise ran through me as a stream of Korean filled my ear. He adjusted a setting on his phone, and suddenly, English replaced the foreign words.

"Mother, this is Priya," I heard CJ say. "The girl I told you about."

Gathering myself, I folded my hands in a respectful Indian namaste and bowed. His mother smiled warmly and mirrored my gesture. I repeated it, but CJ stopped me with a grin, gently grasping my hand. "It's fine," he whispered.

"You are very beautiful," his mother said, her tone filled with kindness. Heat rose to my cheeks. Never in my life had I been complimented in such a way.

"I am nothing in comparison to you," I replied earnestly, and it was the absolute truth. She was breathtaking, the very embodiment of elegance. Looking at her, I understood why they said Korean beauty knew no bounds.

CJ translated my words, and to my surprise, his mother blushed, waving a hand as if to shush me. I smiled at her affection.

"She doesn't look old," his mother complained to CJ. "She looks much younger than you!"

And I bit my lip, controlling myself from spilling the truth. But CJ spoke on my behalf. "Age is nothing mom. She is not just beautiful on the outside, but also on the inside," he was saying. "Mother, do you know she has adopted three children with her sister? She takes care of them single-handedly."

His mother's jaw slackened in shock, even though I distinctly remember him mentioning this to his mother before. I fidgeted under her gaze, feeling suddenly exposed. As always, CJ noticed everything.

"You have?" his mother asked, her voice serious.

I hesitated, then nodded.

"You are brave and kind," she said, admiration flickering in her eyes. "No wonder Mirae has fallen head over heels for you."

I stiffened. He had?

His mother continued, "When I asked him to stay away from you, he refused. And now, I understand why."

I turned to CJ in shock. He had defied his mother? For me?

"Even his father was furious," she added. "I have never seen him so angry, but Mirae did not budge."

"His father?" I asked, confused.

"There," his mother gestured subtly.

I followed her gaze and found Mr Choi Man-Young standing among a small group of distinguished men. But his gaze was locked on me. No, he was not just watching, he was glowering at me. Loathing darkened his features.

He caught my stare and, without hesitation, strode toward us.

CJ tensed. He leaned toward me and whispered urgently, "I invited Chirag and Alex to keep you company," his gaze flickered toward them. "Go to them." Then, in an even lower voice, "Avoid my biological father at all costs."

I hesitated, but then obeyed, weaving through the murmuring crowd.

As I passed, whispers trailed in my wake, which I could understand, thanks to the listening device now attached to my ear.

'Who is she?'

'What does she think of herself?'

'Did you see how CJ was clinging to her?'

And the most shocking of all: 'CJ introduced her to his mother. I cannot believe it!'

I tried to block them out as I joined Chirag and Alex.

"What's going on between you and Mr Choi?" Alex asked immediately.

"He told me he likes me," I answered honestly, omitting certain… err… details.

Chirag stiffened but nodded.

"Well, I can't blame the man," Alex boomed with laughter. "What's not to like in a girl like you?"

I flushed again.

"Seriously, if I were twenty years younger, I'd have tried my luck too," Alex winked. "Oh, you have no drink. Let me get you one." And with that, he was off, still laughing.

I always liked Alex very much. He was so informal, causal, and nice. His laughter always made me smile.

"I am sorry," Chirag spoke, cutting in my thoughts.

"What?" I asked, surprised that he was speaking to me. He had been ignoring me for a week, ever since he told me he liked me.

"For how I behaved. Of course, you are entitled to like whoever you want. I like you, it is my problem," he shrugged.

"I am sorry Chirag," I started. "I don't want to lose you as a friend, seriously. But I am not looking for anything serious with anyone. CJ and I, well, it is temporary. He likes me, I like him. But as you know, I will go back in some time, and well, he has an empire to run."

Chirag's eyebrows shot up at this.

"Yes, he told me his truth," I laughed. "He told me that he asked you to not tell me. So much of a friend you are, huh!" I teased.

"Sorry," was all Chirag said.

"So, you will leave my son?" a voice spoke softly from behind me, and I jumped.

It was Mr Choi Man-Young, and Chirag bowed so low in front of him that I swear he could lick his thighs.

"Leave us," Mr Choi Man-Young dismissed Chirag. "Walk with me, will you?" he ordered, and without waiting for an answer he started to walk.

I looked around, CJ was nowhere to be found.

"Now," Mr Choi Man-Young demanded. And I obeyed as firstly, I did not wish to create a scene, and secondly, I was not scared. I had dealt with worse men in my life than Mr Choi Man-Young.

"What are you up to with my son?" he demanded.

"Nothing," I shrugged.

"I can see what you are getting," he spoke, eyeing me from top to toe, "the dress you wear is loud enough to state that."

I pursed my lips but did not reply.

"Why are you toying with my son?" he demanded.

"I like CJ," I replied simply but defiantly. "And I am not toying with him. I respect him, more than he respects you, for that matter."

Mr Choi Man-Young looked furious, but he didn't reply to my comment. Damn! If he had replied, I would have given him a piece of my mind. How dare he insult CJ all those weeks ago in cafeteria!

"What is your price to stay away from him? He's very distracted since you came, and I don't like it," he hissed.

"What?" I was getting more confused by the second. "He is never distracted, he is very focused."

"He has even started disobeying my direct orders," he huffed. "All because of you!"

I wondered what he did this time… Was my hunch right about my attendance at this party?

Anyway, I wasn't going to give Mr. Choi Man-Young the satisfaction of guessing. So instead, I spoke, "If he is disobeying you, then you must be asking something incredibly stupid," I snapped. "And if he is standing up for himself, then I think it is about time."

If his nostrils could flare more, I swear he would have burnt me with fire.

"Just name your price," he spoke through gritted teeth.

"I am not sellable," I crossed my arms and replied.

His eyebrows shot up at this, but then a grin appeared. The grin made him look less handsome, less like a billionaire, and more like a shrewd, cunning fox willing to rip me to shreds.

"Everyone has a price," he added with a wink.

"Not me," I stressed.

"Just name your price and leave my son," he hissed.

"I am leaving in a few weeks, he will forget me in some time, why are you even bothering?" I asked seriously.

"Name your price and leave him now… better, leave this country tonight," he insisted. "I will pay you whatever you want. I will even give you a million dollars if you fly out tonight."

I stared at him in shock.

"Here," he spoke as he pulled out his cheque book and started to sign it.

"Write your price," he stressed as he thrusted the cheque book and pen in my hand.

I was taken aback. I wanted to go, but he persisted.

"Write or I will force you to," he threatened.

And I don't know why, I saw shadows move in the surroundings.

I took the pen and stared at the cheque.

What the hell!

"Name your price and go," he hissed. The men who were shadows grew closer.

And I wrote. As I wrote, a malicious grin spread on his face that was devious.

"Everyone has a price," he smirked as he made to take the cheque book once I was done, but CJ took it instead. I didn't know he was standing behind me, and his father was teasing him with that last comment.

CJ was stunned, shocked that I have named a price. He looked furious at his father, but more shocked at me.

But I just eyed the cheque book pointedly. So, he looked down and read my price.

He laughed wearily as he threw the cheque book at his father and held me in his arms, and spoke, "Now you know why I chose her, Choi Man-Young. You cannot buy her, father," he spat the last word with a scathing look, "but I can, with this," and he grabbed my neck, and kissed me furiously on lips, making the world melt away.

33

Love, care & patience

When we broke apart, Mr Choi Man-Young was nowhere to be seen. CJ glanced outside and said, "His entourage is gone."

"You mean he left his own house?" I asked, looking out as well.

CJ just shrugged carelessly, as if he didn't care about his father leaving at all.

"He said you have been very distracted, and disobeying him since I arrived," I informed CJ, to which he just grinned.

"Well? Have you?" I insisted.

"Yeah, I have been spending quite a lot of time in bed lately," he shrugged in an off-hand way, rolling his eyes in a rather cute, dramatic way.

I blushed…

"And, apart from that?" I grinned, still blushing.

"He did ask me to stop seeing you. Asked my mother too, like Mom told you," he continued. I nodded.

"And…" he paused.

"And he asked you today not to bring me to this party?" I asked.

He raised his eyebrows. "How did you know?"

"I guessed it," I shrugged.

He bent down and kissed me again, so passionately that for a moment I forgot where we were.

"What was that for?" I asked, breathless, as he pulled back.

"For being so smart," he pecked my lips again.

"Oh, that," I smiled, dazed.

"Anyway, yes, he asked me not to bring you here to Mom's house!" CJ nodded.

"So you disobeyed him, and he left his own house because I'm here?" I clarified.

"He doesn't live here," CJ said in a venomous tone. "This is my mom's house. She lives here with my father. Well, technically, not my father… he's my mother's brother. But he raised me, and when I was little, I started calling him Dad. He never corrected me because he is my father for all intents and purposes. He runs the European division of ZenTel. I guess my bio dad put him in charge of Europe to keep me away from him. But Mr Choi Man-Young doesn't realize that bonds don't break that easily."

"So, when you said your dad asked you to go to London?" I asked, piecing things together.

"It was actually him, my maternal uncle. But…"

"A father to you," I finished for him.

He nodded. "My mother still loves my bio dad. Despite everything, his antics, his carefree lifestyle, she's still waiting for him to change and come back to her," he sighed. "But I know he won't."

I had no words for that.

"A child needs a father, Priya," he said simply.

"I'm glad you found one in your other dad," I offered a small smile.

"Every child needs a father, Priya," he repeated, his voice weighted with meaning.

And somehow, I knew he was talking about my children. I looked down, hoping my eyes wouldn't betray my thoughts.

"Did you really mean what you wrote in the cheque?" he asked. "I heard everything. Do you really think I'll forget you that easily when you leave?" He placed a finger under my chin, lifting my face. "Or are you telling me you'll forget me that easily?"

"I would never forget you, CJ," I whispered. "I…" I wanted to tell him so much, but I hesitated. How could I possibly put it into words?

"Your price is love, care, and patience," he said, repeating what I had written in the cheque. "I will give you all of that."

"I know," I whispered, but then, in a rush, I blurted, "But I'm too broken for you… too poor, too much baggage. How can you be with someone like me? You need someone whole, not someone like me. You have no idea about my past, and if you knew, you would hate me, CJ!"

"Damn it!" he cursed. For a moment, I thought it was because of my words, but then he rubbed his ear and groaned. "You were speaking slowly before, using small words. I could understand you. But just now, I didn't catch a damn thing you said."

And despite everything, I laughed.

I looked around. We were alone. I kissed him lightly on the lips.

"Later," I whispered. "Let's go inside. I think people are missing you." And with that, I pushed him back inside.

34

Kisses & permissions

I had feared that his mother would hate me, but to my surprise, she loved me. She spent most of her time with me, talking, fussing over little things, and making sure I ate whatever was offered. And while I understood her perfectly, thanks to CJ's listening device, I used CJ, Chirag or Alex for translating my words to her.

It felt as if she were my mother, not his. And every time she showed me even the smallest act of care, a pang of longing hit me. I often wondered how different my life would have been if my own mother had lived. Would things have been any better?

Every time that thought crossed my mind, my heart sank. But every time, she lifted me back up with her warmth. She was such a loving, caring mother, and I couldn't help but question whether I was even half as good to my own children. I doubted it, given the weight of responsibilities I carried, but I was sure Dhriti took after women like her.

His mother retired for the night around ten, and most of the other elders followed soon after. By eleven, only twenty of us remained. Some were drinking, others dancing, and the rest just lazing around, but everyone seemed to be enjoying themselves.

CJ glanced around and sighed, "These parties never end on time."

Thanks to my earpiece, I could understand everything people were saying, no matter the language. And now, more than ever, I wanted one for myself.

"It'll end soon," I assured him.

"Yeah?" he grinned at me. "I want to show you the house, but not with everyone here."

"Later," I mused, then leaned in and whispered in his ear, "After all, we have the whole night to ourselves."

His eyes widened at the suggestion in my tone, and he swallowed.

"But I want that to happen now," he murmured, pulling me close and squeezing my waist knowingly.

I giggled and pulled away. I had watched enough mean-girl dramas with Dhriti to know that any romantic moment at a party like this could easily be caught on camera and circulated.

"Hey, CJ!" a girl called out. "Let's play a game."

"Yeah, which one?" he responded, still holding onto me.

Suggestions started flying around: charades, spin the bottle, fishbowl.

Fishbowl caught CJ's interest, but then someone suggested truth or dare. He looked at me with amusement, and I shook my head playfully.

"Don't worry, I'll save you," he grinned, and we eventually settled on spin the bottle with truth or dare.

We all formed a circle, with CJ on one side of me and Alex on the other, Chirag next to Alex, and the rest scattered around. Then the game began.

The bottle first landed on a girl who introduced herself as Sheena, her Western name, apparently. She chose to dare and was told to kiss someone. Predictably, she picked CJ. She leaned in and kissed him full on the lips, burning a hole in my heart. He pulled back quickly, offering her a polite smile.

"Sorry about that," he murmured under his breath as the game continued.

Next, it landed on a guy who chose truth. His question: 'Who is your dream girl?' His answer: a girl named Soo Ya. The room erupted in cheers, and a few girls exchanged texts excitedly. Feeling out of place, I started chatting randomly with Chirag and Alex, who, like me, were outsiders in this group.

The game went on, mostly revolving around their close-knit circle, making it hard for me to relate. Then another girl kissed CJ. Chirag got up and danced, and he was surprisingly good. Then another girl kissed CJ. Then Alex sang a Celine Dion song, making everyone laugh and swoon. Then another girl kissed CJ.

By the time the fifth girl leaned in for a kiss, my blood was boiling. Sensing my frustration, CJ took my hand, as if he could feel me on the verge of walking out.

Then the bottle landed on CJ.

"Truth or dare?" everyone chorused.

"How about both?" he smirked.

Cheers erupted, but I interjected curtly, "Alright, truth first. Do you enjoy it when all these girls fall over you and kiss you? Don't you think they should at least ask for permission?"

CJ raised an eyebrow. "That's two questions," he mused. "But no, I don't enjoy being kissed without permission, though it's fine since it's just a game."

"Game hoga tere liye, baaki mere liye toh ye saari chudel hain..." I muttered under my breath, anger and jealousy simmering within me. (Translation: This might be a game for you, but to me, all these girls are witches.)

Chirag, who understood Hindi, nearly choked on his drink, laughing.

"What did she say?" CJ asked suspiciously.

Chirag glanced between us and, under CJ's scrutinizing gaze, hesitated before answering, "She said it might be a game for you, but it doesn't feel like one to her."

I exhaled in relief that he didn't expose my 'witch' comment. CJ, however, seemed to catch on to the mistranslation but didn't press further.

"So, dare," one of CJ's friends prompted, shifting the attention back to the game.

"Yes, dare," CJ chuckled. "What should I do?"

I muttered under my breath, "I dare you to kiss one of these girls," surprising even myself with the venom in my voice. I quickly lowered my head and stayed silent.

CJ's friend, who seemed particularly close to him, gave him a cocky look. I wondered why he hadn't spoken to me throughout the party. I saw him speak to CJ a few times, but CJ didn't introduce me to him.

"Why don't you do something you've always wanted to do but never done in public?" his friend challenged with a wiggle of his eyebrows.

CJ pouted. "I have no problem doing whatever I want in public."

"Oh, in that case, I dare you to do it while standing on this table," his friend added.

CJ laughed, "Let's spare the table. My mother wouldn't like people standing on it."

But the group started cheering. I pulled out my phone, ready to text Dhriti, when CJ's voice rang out.

"Many girls have kissed me tonight and before, but that's not a real kiss. That's not how you kiss," he grinned. The girls in the room sat up in anticipation. "I've never kissed anyone properly in public. So here it goes."

Anger flared in me. He was going to kiss someone, right now?

I turned to leave, but he caught my hand and pulled me back. I looked in his eyes and of course, he was going to kiss me in public!

"Do I have your permission to kiss you right now?" he asked seriously, his eyes locked onto mine.

A chorus of hoots and cheers filled the room. I felt the heat rush to my face as I glanced around… everyone had their phones out.

"No," I whispered. "Please, no," I shook my head, even as every fibre in my body screamed 'yes.'

CJ sighed, pressed a brief kiss to my cheek, and whispered before pulling away, "I just love how possessive you are getting!"

My eyes widened at his words. Was I really getting possessive of him? But he wasn't mine to possess, or was he?

"Sorry, Jay," he addressed his friend. "She said no."

More hoots and laughter erupted.

"Tough luck, my friend," Jay teased.

And the game went on. But at least after that, no other girl kissed him.

35

A thousand years

I was one of the last people to have the bottle land on me. And when it did, Jay casually turned to me and asked, "Priya, truth or dare?"

I could tell he was someone who spoke English fluently, just like most of the people in his group.

"Whatever," I shrugged.

"How about both, then?" he laughed. "Like him. After all, he is your..."

"Nothing," I cut in swiftly. "He is my boss, that's it."

CJ's eyebrows lifted ever so slightly at my words.

Jay smirked. "So, truth first. Why didn't you let him kiss you? Any girl in the world would have fallen if he had asked that sincerely. I mean I would have kissed him if he had looked at me like that."

I met his gaze, unwavering, though I did smile at his last comment. "Because, firstly, I am not just any girl, and secondly, some things should remain private."

"So, you have kissed him in private?" a girl chimed in, her voice teasing. "Oooh, CJ! What else have you two done in private?"

"Oh, shut up," CJ retorted with an airy laugh.

"Alright, dare time," Jay announced.

"I dare you to take off your dress," one of the drunk girls giggled, one of the same girls who had kissed CJ earlier.

I stiffened, momentarily taken aback, but Jay waved it off. "No, not that," he said, then turned to CJ, watching him intently. "How about this? Write down your true feelings, whatever they are, and share them with someone you care about in this group. Privately, of course," he added the last part with a knowing wink.

CJ straightened slightly at the suggestion.

I glanced at him and, under my breath, asked, "Jay is your best friend, isn't he?"

"Yes," CJ admitted with a grin, "and if we'll have a western ceremony, then he'll be the best man at our wedding."

My head snapped toward him at the words 'our wedding'. I swallowed, blinking rapidly.

"At *my* wedding," he corrected quickly.

Sensing the shift in the air, Jay clapped his hands together. "How about we all play fishbowl and write something about the people here?"

"Sounds good," CJ said, regaining his composure.

But the words 'our wedding' still echoed in my mind.

"People should write in English," I murmured to Jay, "or I'll be the only one whose note is in English, and then it won't be anonymous."

"Fair point," Jay nodded before announcing the rule to the group, of course to people who could write English.

Everyone took to the activity with enthusiasm, scribbling their thoughts onto slips of paper. I wrote something for everyone, even though I had only just learned most of their names, keeping my notes light and polite: I like your shoes. Your dress is nice. This colour brings out your eyes.

I left a warm, friendly note for Chirag, another for Alex, and then… a small but heartfelt one for CJ.

Despite writing so many, I finished quickly, dropping my slips into the bowl before heading off to get some water.

Then the game began.

Jay shuffled the bowl and pulled out the first slip. It was mine. "Dear Mia, your dress is gorgeous. Red suits you."

Mia giggled, blushing as she took the note and sat back.

Jay drew another, read it, then silently pocketed it.

A third note read, "Priya, your smile brightens my day. Always keep smiling."

I smiled at the words, thanking Alex, I knew it was from him, before sitting back.

CJ picked up a slip, read it, then pocketed it with a grimace. He muttered something to Jay, who quietly handed over the note he had pocketed earlier. CJ read it, his frown deepening.

Another note read, "CJ, I love you. Marry me, please. XOXO."

CJ laughed, though the frown lingered.

A few more notes followed; polite messages meant for others. But now and then, Jay would slip a note to CJ in silence, and each time, CJ read them with growing intensity.

One after another, confessions of love directed at CJ surfaced. Then came Chirag's note for me: an apology for what had happened, a reminder that he truly cherished our friendship. I hugged him softly and sat back.

Then, another note which Jay quietly slipped to CJ. And another. Jay kept passing them along, and with each one, CJ's expression darkened. And with every note I wondered what the notes say.

Finally, Jay pulled out CJ's note for me. His eyebrows shot up as he read it, his jaw dropping slightly, his ears turning the faintest shade of red. Then, without a word, he walked over and handed it to me, whispering, "If you want a translation, I'll do it gladly."

I looked down at the slip. It was written entirely in Korean symbols, but even without understanding a single word, I knew what it meant.

I nodded, my fingers tightening around the note.

People clamoured to know what it said, but Jay simply shrugged. "It is labelled 'private', guys."

Laughter erupted.

Then, another love note for CJ.

And then… mine.

Jay read it despite the word 'private' written on top. He grinned broadly at first, but then his expression shifted, a frown flickering across his face. He handed it to CJ without a word. Everyone again demanded to know but Jay just shrugged.

CJ pulled out his phone, clicked a photo of my note and I knew he was translating it.

It read,

"My dear CJ, if only you knew how much I longed to declare to the world what you mean to me with that kiss. But I couldn't, not because I didn't want to, but because some feelings are too precious to be put on display. Your love is my sanctuary, a cocoon I have wrapped around myself, and I never wish to leave it.

Words will never be enough to tell you what your love, your care, your very presence mean to me. But know this… you are everything I want, everything I will ever want.

But I know our paths will part one day. I know this love, no matter how deep, may not have a future. But please, don't ask me to explain, because I won't. Just know this:

To me, you are, 'a thousand years and more.'"

The game continued, but CJ stopped reading the quiet notes Jay handed him.

Once all the notes had been read, CJ clapped his hands together and announced, "One last game for the evening… a guessing game." A mischievous glint flickered in his eyes.

Jay moved beside me, subtly gesturing for Alex and Chirag to shift, creating a more private space. Leaning in, he asked, "Why are your paths parting ways?"

I met his gaze briefly before shaking my head. Meanwhile, CJ's voice rang through the room.

"Whoever guesses correctly will win the latest model of ZenTel's smartphone, so exclusive that even I don't know its market price yet because it hasn't been launched!"

A collective cheer erupted, excitement buzzing through the group.

"What's the question?" a girl asked eagerly.

CJ smirked. "What does the phrase 'a thousand years and more' mean? Priya here will confirm the right answer."

All eyes turned to me.

"Why her?" a girl asked with venom dripping from her tone. "Why is she so special?"

And CJ lost it.

"She is special because despite you all behaving like absolute bitches, she has written nothing but nice things about you, for each of you. And what have you all written? Only bad things, things to put her down, things that don't define her, but you… you all should be ashamed of yourself. She is special because she *is* special, and this is the last time, anyone," and CJ glared at the girls in the group, "anyone insults her!"

Stunned silence met these words but my body was covered in goosebumps.

"Still think you should part ways?" Jay whispered in my ears.

And I stared at him in shock.

"Chill CJ, let's play your guessing game…" Jay spoke to him. "This is usual, let it be…"

CJ huffed, then his eyes met mine. I nodded solemnly, and then I smiled.

"Fine," CJ huffed again. "The game then. Phrase 'a thousand years' what does it mean?" he repeated.

Jay leaned back, murmuring, "You can answer me later."

"Can we use our phones to search?" someone asked, already reaching for their device.

CJ nodded, finally smiling now. "Go ahead, use any source you like. Just tell me what 'a thousand years' truly means."

The guesses began pouring in.

"It's the literal number of years," one boy suggested.

I shook my head.

"It means forever," a girl chimed in.

Another shake.

Silence settled over the group as they considered.

"I think it means eternal love," Jay proposed.

I shook my head once more.

Then, after a long pause, Chirag spoke. "I remember there's a song called A Thousand Years by Christina Perri. It was in that vampire movie… Twilight."

My lips parted slightly, my breath catching. *Damn it, Chirag.*

CJ's gaze flickered with intrigue. "Is he right?" he asked me.

I nodded and everyone cheered for Chirag.

"Then let's play it," Jay declared, moving to the stereo. Moments later, the familiar melody began to drift through the room.

As the first notes filled the air, CJ extended his hand toward me. Without hesitation, I placed mine in his, letting him guide me to my feet. His other hand found its place around my waist, and he swayed me gently to the rhythm.

One by one, others joined in, moving in time with the music, but my world had already faded to just him and me.

"Talk to me," CJ whispered near my ear.

"Let's not talk," I murmured back, resting my head against his shoulder.

In his embrace, I melted… forgetting the world, forgetting the loneliness looming on the horizon. And most of all, forgetting that once, this had been my favourite song, a melody that made me dream of forever love.

And now that I had it, I couldn't hold onto it forever.

36

Moments & lifetime

I never got the chance to see his mother's house that night. The party lasted until dawn, fading only when CJ's mother woke at six in the morning. One by one, the guests trickled out, murmuring sleepy goodbyes as the first rays of sunlight touched the sky.

She offered to let us stay, but CJ stretched, stifling a yawn, and said he had work to do. "We should head home too," he added.

Home! My heart skipped a beat at the word, and his mother's smile widened knowingly. She pulled me into a warm embrace, holding me close as she whispered, "I am so happy."

But I wasn't happy. I was dying inside.

The drive back was quiet, the roads empty in the stillness of Sunday morning. CJ drove faster than usual, as if rushing against time itself. When we finally reached, I slipped off my heels the moment we stepped inside… what bliss it was to be barefoot again. His note remained tucked safely in my purse, untouched but ever-present.

I headed straight to the shower, half expecting him to join me. But when I emerged, wrapped in a bathrobe, I found him standing on the balcony, his gaze lost on the horizon.

"You're leaving on Thursday?" he asked the moment I stepped out.

"I am. You know that," I replied softly.

"When will you be back?"

"Tuesday."

A pause. Then, as if making a decision right there and then, he said, "I'll come this time. Stay with you."

I blinked, caught off guard. A laugh escaped me, unbidden. CJ, the billionaire CJ, staying in my tiny two-bedroom apartment? The thought alone was absurd. With my three children and sister, we were already pressed for space, squeezing together in a home that had long outgrown us. What would happen if he was added to the mix?

"What?" he asked, frowning slightly.

"My house is small. My life is small," I started, but he dismissed my words with a shake of his head.

Reaching for the listening piece in my ear, he gently removed it and placed it into his own. I watched as he mumbled something in Korean, his voice a low murmur of determination.

I frowned. "English?" I prompted, smiling despite myself.

"Will make one more," he repeated pointing at his earpiece, eyes unwavering.

I sighed. "Yeah, well… I'd be gone by then, wouldn't I?"

That made him straighten. His gaze locked onto mine, intense, unwavering. "And in any case, I like your voice. Not the mechanical translation. I think I understand you just enough to know what you mean."

Then, with quiet certainty, he said, very slowly in English, "I … want you… to… come back."

I inhaled, steadying myself, "I will be back."

His jaw tensed, and he continued, "I want you to… always… come back."

Without waiting for my response, he turned and disappeared inside, only to return moments later with his tablet. Then he spoke, his voice firm, the translation appearing on the screen.

"I don't care if your family is back in India. You have to come back to me. Or I will come to you. We can live there. I don't care. But you have to come back to me."

I stared at the words, my heart tightening.

Mistaking my silence, he chuckled dryly as he added, "So, this is it, huh? I am building a home in someone who is already planning to leave…?"

His words hit me like a stone but I didn't say anything to his confession. What could you say when someone calls you his 'home'?

"I'm leaving for India, forever when I come next," I said, my voice quieter now, but steady. "I have a family there. They are my responsibility. I will never choose you, or anyone, over them. And you have your life here… you also have your priorities… So, CJ, we have two options… either we have these twenty days together, and then we part ways, or I leave now and never come back. The choice is yours."

Silence.

CJ stared at me for a long time, his eyes heavy with exhaustion, with unshed tears. And then, slowly, he exhaled, his shoulders dropping in reluctant acceptance.

He mumbled something under his breath, and I glanced at the translation.

"Twenty days, huh."

I nodded.

Then, barely above a whisper, he asked, "What about a thousand years?"

A small smile touched my lips as I reached for the belt of my bathrobe, my fingers toying with the knot. "Haven't you heard?" I murmured. "You can live a lifetime in a single moment. So what are a thousand years?"

And with that, I let the robe part slightly, baring my skin to him, to the quiet ache between us.

His gaze darkened, trailing over me with quiet reverence. He muttered something in Korean, his voice laced with desire, the word 'balcony' slipping through.

I knew what he meant.

He wanted me here, then and there.

And yes, we did make full use of the balcony that morning… of course, only in places where prying eyes couldn't see.

37

A part of me, a part of you

The next week passed in a haze of exhaustion and adrenaline. Our prototype entered its testing phase, and we spent hours on end debugging, fine-tuning, and pushing ourselves past the limits of fatigue. Despite the chaos, I couldn't ignore the shifting atmosphere in the office. The women who once merely disliked me now seethed with open hostility, while the men who had once eyed me with curiosity now steered clear. The message was clear: I belonged to CJ.

But I didn't care. I was drowning in work, barely finding time to melt into CJ's arms at home.

Before I knew it, Thursday arrived, and I was back on a plane to India. This time, the separation stung deeper than before. CJ drove me to the airport, using his usual privileges to stay by my side until the very last moment. He held me close, his embrace desperate, refusing to let go until the flight attendant tapped him on the shoulder, forcing me to board.

And then I was gone.

Back home, I threw myself into my family, revelling in every moment with my children. We went out, we laughed, we created memories, yet something inside me ached with a loneliness I had never felt before. CJ was always in the background of my mind, a whisper of warmth I could no longer reach.

I replayed us in my head like a punishment, every laugh, every touch, every moment. And it was nothing short of torture…

"Why don't we all move to Seoul?" Rohan, my eldest son, asked at dinner on Sunday.

Dhriti immediately shot down the idea. "Your mother will be back in fifteen days, and we will continue to live here."

"But I don't like it here," Rohan argued. "The house is too small, the school is horrible, and what college do you expect me to go to? Despite my grades, I'll never make it to IIT or anything good, I mean how can we pay for it?"

My heart clenched. Of course, I couldn't afford IIT. Hell, I could barely afford any decent college at all.

"We'll take student loans, like we planned," Dhriti countered. "No one is moving to a country where we know no one."

"Mom knows CJ," Dhara, our daughter, chimed in brightly. "I like him. When can we meet him?"

"Never," Dhriti snapped.

"But…" Rohan moaned.

"No means no. Now eat." And with that, silence settled over the table.

I think I have had sex in the last ten days more than the number of years in my age, and while it was not the first thing on my mind, my thoughts often drifted to the times when CJ had caressed my body, nipped at sensitive places, and made love to me so tenderly that every time those memories surfaced, I had to press my legs together to regain control.

"You will come back, right?" Dhriti asked as I loaded my bags into the cab.

I nodded, pulling her into a hug. "I will always come back to my family."

"Then why are you taking that?" she asked, her voice sharp. "I saw you take it out of the box."

"I have to tell him, Dhriti. I owe him that much."

She nodded, though I could see the lack of understanding in her eyes. "I think it's too late to warn you, but please… don't break your heart, okay? It's terrifying how someone can become your whole world and then vanish, leaving you lost inside your own life."

I knew she was talking about her own heartbreak, the one from which she never healed fully, but I didn't comment.

I smiled faintly. "My heart is here, don't worry." And with that, I left.

When I landed, CJ was exactly where I had left him. Waiting. His presence surrounded me, steady and warm, as he guided me through immigration and out into the world that was ours.

I was always surprised how everyone knew him and didn't ask any questions about his unnecessary presence.

The car ride was filled with talk of work, but as soon as we stepped inside our home, silence enveloped us.

"Did you ask your family?" CJ asked as soon as we crossed the threshold.

I didn't answer. Instead, I dropped my bag, closed the distance between us, and wrapped myself around him. I inhaled him, his scent, his strength, his unshakable presence. I wanted to soak him into my very being, make him a part of me so permanent that no distance could take him away.

We stayed in the apartment that day, and then we resumed work the next day, and by the end of the week, our prototype was flawless. The launch was imminent, another storm of meetings and stress, and CJ was so occupied that twice I found myself alone in the office, waiting for him past 11 PM. I didn't mind staying in office and working, but I was just not used to it now without him.

When the weekend arrived, he took me out.

"This trip was meant to happen when you first came back from India, but of course, other things took precedence then," he admitted sheepishly. And I remembered what took precedence, a luxurious bath in that hotel's bathtub. "But now, finally, its time."

We went to N Seoul Tower, a breathtaking place that made me feel both insignificant and infinite at once. Thousands of love locks lined the railings, promises sealed in metal. CJ bought two.

As I scribbled my wish onto mine, *I wish we could be together, forever,* I saw him writing something on his own. But when I asked what he wished for, he only sighed.

"Nothing new. Always the same."

I reached into my bag, pulling out the note he had left for me during the fishbowl game. "Did you mean this?" I asked, handing it to him.

"Did you read it?" he asked, his voice unreadable.

"I tried," I admitted. "But I don't think I truly understood it. Will you read it to me?"

He nodded, but before he could begin, I hesitated. "CJ… is there anything you haven't told me?"

He frowned. "What do you mean?"

"You've told me about your family, your life… but is there something more?"

He shook his head. "Nothing left to tell."

I braced myself. "Then read your note to me."

CJ pulled out his listening device and placed it over my ear, switching the setting so I could hear his words in English.

"Priya," he murmured, his voice thick with emotion. "My Priya. I have no words to express how I feel for you. I still remember the first moment I saw you, sitting across from me. My breath caught, my focus shattered. I knew, in that instant, what you would mean to me.

"I have spent my life feeling lost, alone. People treat me with reverence, with careful distance, but you… you don't. I see no calculation in your eyes, no worship. Only respect, only care, the same care you offer even to the driver who opens your door.

"You are what I have been missing. And from the moment I held you, kissed you, touched you in ways only I can, I have felt whole.

"You always say our worlds don't meet, you are an Indian and I am a Korean. And that you have to go back… but you should know this: when you'll leave, you are not just leaving this country alone. You are taking a part of me with you. A part I don't think I can live without."

Tears slipped silently down my cheeks. He turned away, staring out at the city stretched beneath us.

I had no words. None that could match his.

So instead, I sat up straight and reached for the device, gesturing for him to take it back.

He needed it now.

He needed to understand what I was about to say.

And he needed to understand why this, us, could never last forever.

38

A sad story but a story nonetheless

I heaved a shaky sigh and reached for his hand, gripping it tightly as if it were the only thing keeping me from falling apart.

"Promise me, you won't interrupt," I whispered, my voice barely above a breath.

He nodded, his gaze steady but questioning.

"And promise me," I continued, my throat tightening, "once you hear the story, you won't fire me or tell anyone. I don't think I could survive in this world if the word got out." My voice cracked at the end, betraying my desperation.

His eyes darkened, but he nodded again, slower this time.

"Promise me for my children," I begged, my fingers digging into his.

His jaw tightened before he finally spoke, "I swear on my mother."

I exhaled deeply, pressing my trembling lips together.

And then, I began.

"Let me tell you a story. A sad story, but a story nonetheless." I looked toward the horizon, the weight of the past pressing down on me.

"Long ago, a little girl lived happily with her parents. Her mother was doting, or at least, that's how she remembers it. They were poor, her father was a sweeper, or something like that in a school but she was happy. She had everything she needed." I swallowed. "But then, when she was eight, her mother died."

CJ stiffened, his grip tightening around my hand, but he remained silent. I knew he knew it was my story because my mother died too when I was eight, but he waited.

I paused, inhaled sharply, and pushed forward.

"Her father remarried. At first, the new mother was kind, but only in front of him. When he wasn't looking, she treated the little girl like filth. Soon, she had two sons of her own, and they became her world. The little girl became a burden. She used to go to the school where her father worked, you know that girl has semantic memory, i.e. she never forgets anything she had heard or read, and that became her strength. She was very intelligent, sharp, could have great future. But then, when she was eleven, her father died too."

A deep silence stretched between us, thick and suffocating.

"She was alone," I continued, my voice hollow. "Alone with a woman who despised her. She endured it all… the beatings, the taunts, the neglect, because she had no choice.

With three children to care for and no money, her stepmother moved in with her so-called brother. He was single, well-off. But now, when she looks back, she knows he couldn't have been her brother. Because they lived in the same room, while all three children were crammed into another.

He worked as a peon in a college. Her stepmother cleaned utensils in strangers' homes to survive. And the girl… she was nothing but an extra mouth to feed."

I clenched my hands together, the tremble spreading through my body.

"So, when she was about twelve, maybe a little younger, she doesn't remember anymore, she got her first period. And that was the day they decided to marry her off."

CJ's body jerked violently. A sharp inhale, but no words.

"Her so-called uncle used his position to steal another girl's identity… identity of an exceptionally bright god-gifted student who had died due to some mental health issues shortly after graduating. She had no family left, no one to ask questions. It was safe, or so they said. So, he stole her birth certificate, her degree, her name. And within days, that twelve-year-old girl became an eighteen-year-old woman.

Her stepmother and uncle burned every trace of her real life. Every document, every picture, every proof of who she truly was. And within months, she was married off…

To a man over thirty."

A shudder ran through me.

CJ's grip on my hand became almost painful, but I welcomed it.

"She had her first child at thirteen." My voice broke, and I let the tears spill freely. "She nearly died in childbirth. But her husband didn't care. He used her, abused her, treated her like she was nothing more than a body for his pleasure.

And soon, she was pregnant again.

But this time, she was so frail, so weak, she could barely stand. She was bedridden. And when she was of no use to him anymore, he left her. Pregnant. With a baby not even a year old."

CJ's sharp hiss cut through the air, but I was too lost in the past to stop now.

"He walked away once... but she kept on reliving that moment over and over again..." I sighed. "They had been renting a small room in the house of a kind family. The family had a sixteen-year-old daughter who took care of the baby when she couldn't even lift her head. The doctor who helped deliver her second child saw what was happening. You know that doctor was an MBBS student back then, working in a government camp. The doctor in charge had left her to take care of the poor patients. She wasn't much older than this girl, and maybe that's why the girl felt safe. She let out her feelings... years of silent misery poured out in front of another girl who, for the first time in a long while, showed her some kindness. The young doctor listened quietly, her hands gently tending to the girl and her eyes holding back the ache of helplessness. She understood the danger, the urgency. The husband could return at any moment.

So the doctor asked, 'I cannot save you from what he may do to you. But I can save you from dying in childbirth again.'

And the girl, broken, terrified, agreed. Agreed to a procedure she couldn't even understand back then, only that it would ensure she never endured pregnancy again."

CJ's face was like stone.

"She was only fourteen. And she was broken and alone... So alone that she had no one but herself to pick up the pieces and stitch herself together..." My voice was a whisper now. "Fourteen, but legally, she was twenty. And she knew she had to fight for her children.

So she studied.

She studied with the landlord's daughter, learning everything she could. The landlord's daughter was not interested in studies, so she studied everything and taught the landlord's daughter. And in doing so, she knew more than any teenager did. By the time she turned fifteen, she applied for an internship at a mobile company's technical support department. She got it." I let out a bitter laugh. "Fifteen years old, working herself to the bone while the family took care of her babies. She paid them nearly everything she earned. It wasn't just gratitude. It was survival."

I blinked rapidly, trying to focus, to stop the tears from clouding my vision.

"But life never lets happiness stay for too long, does it?" My lips curled in a humourless smile.

"The landlord's daughter got pregnant. She was naive, easily manipulated. The boy left, and her parents were furious. They wanted her to give up the child.

But she couldn't.

She had seen that girl raise two children alone. She had seen her fight, and she wanted to fight too.

Her parents blamed the girl for their daughter's 'ruin' and threw them both out."

CJ shut his eyes, his head hanging low, as if he couldn't bear to hear more.

"The girl found a shack to live in with the pregnant sixteen-year-old. By the time her sister, because that's what she had become, gave birth, the girl had worked her way up. She had become the best programmer in the company.

She had money.

Not much, but enough to keep them afloat.

She worked non-stop. And her sister stayed home to raise their three children, one of them her own, two of them the girl's.

The girl became the father.

The sister became the mother.

And together, they raised a family."

CJ exhaled harshly, rubbing his face, but I wasn't done.

"So yeah… that's the story," I whispered. "Of a girl who, on paper, is thirty-two, but in reality, is only twenty-six. A girl who tells the world she has adopted three orphans because the truth is too ugly to bear.

A girl who sometimes dreams of love but knows she can never have it, because any day now, her so-called husband could return and destroy everything she has built.

And because no man deserves a woman who cannot bear his children anymore. A woman who is so broken, so damaged, that she can't even meet her own eyes in the mirror."

CJ's head snapped up. His gaze was fierce, burning with something unreadable.

"Your real name?" he asked, his voice hoarse.

I reached into my bag and pulled out a single sheet of paper, faded, crumpled, the last piece of my stolen identity.

"You know I have nothing of me! I don't even have a photo of my mother. I can't even remember now how she looked like!" I sniffed. "The only thing that survived my step mother's purge," I said, my voice hollow. "My admit card from my last exam. The only proof of who I once was."

I handed it to him.

"My name was Meera Saraswat."

CJ froze. His expression changed, shock, disbelief, something deeper.

"A coincidence, yes, that our names are similar," I murmured, a bitter smile on my lips. "My mother was a devotee of Lord Krishna. Meera was his greatest devotee. She named me after her."

"That's why you hate your name?" he asked softly.

I nodded.

"I cringe every time someone says it. That name destroyed me. The only thing that name gave me was a degree that enabled me to work and find independence. I was not happy before, but what I endured after taking that name is wordless. That man, my so-called husband, that name… ruined my life."

I closed my eyes as horrors of my past flashed in front of my eyes.

Silence.

And then, CJ moved. He closed the distance between us, pulling me into his arms.

"It's okay," he whispered, his breath warm against my skin. "You're safe."

I clung to him.

And for the first time in years, I let myself believe it.

Even if only for a moment.

39

Leaving you... Not!

Whatever CJ had planned for that day went down the drain. He was absolutely quiet throughout our way back, and I wondered if he would just throw me out of the house right away. My heart pounded in my chest, each beat reminding me of the inevitable distance growing between us.

When we walked in, he went straight to the balcony, without sparing me a second glance.

And I didn't know what to do.

I sat on our bed, staring at his back, my vision blurred with unshed tears. He stood there, rigid and unmoving, gazing out at the street as if searching for answers in the bustle it housed. I longed for him to turn around, to say something, anything. But the silence stretched between us, suffocating and endless.

He finally moved, but only to murmur something in Korean, his voice low and unreadable. I could barely make out the words, but I understood what he meant. He was leaving.

And then, he was gone.

The second he stepped out, something inside me cracked. I had never felt this lonely before, not since I started living with Dhriti. The hollowness settled deep within my bones, wrapping around me like a suffocating shroud.

The chef came and cooked lunch, but I barely noticed. I ate in silence, my throat constricting with every bite. Then I waited. Hours passed as I wandered aimlessly around the house, my thoughts a whirlwind of regret, guilt, and the unshakable feeling that I had lost something I could never get back. My tears never stopped; they fell endlessly, soaking my sleeves, my hands, my very existence.

The chef returned for dinner, but still, CJ did not.

As the minutes bled into hours, my heart sank further. He wasn't coming back. The night grew heavier, because every star reminded me of a life that would never come true now.

By 9:30 PM, the realization settled in, cold and final. He had left me. Of course, he had. Why would he stay with someone so broken? Someone who had endured so much pain that love seemed like a distant, unattainable dream? A girl who had carried the weight of motherhood, not by choice, but by circumstance. A woman who had nothing left to offer but scars and burdens.

Tears spilled down my face as my mind replayed every painful moment of my past, every unspoken fear, every reason why I was unworthy of love.

And I wasn't asking him to stay forever… just long enough to feel like I mattered. Just long enough to not feel like I meant nothing. But that didn't happen… he just left!

Slowly, I moved through the house, touching everything as if memorizing it one last time. By 10:30, I could no longer bear it. My hands trembled as I reached for my bag, my body wracked with sobs as I stuffed my things inside. My belongings were scattered everywhere, and it took me longer than it should have to collect them… partly because every few minutes, I broke down again, my body collapsing under the weight of my sorrow.

I have been hurt before… I have been broken to my core… but it hurts differently when the person who gave you your best memories becomes the reason you can't sleep at night.

By midnight, I was fully packed. And I knew what I had to do.

The prototype was ready. Alex had already left for Germany. There was no reason for me to stay. I clutched my last ticket, staring at it through blurry eyes. I would go to the airport and beg them to prepone it. And if they refused, I would wait, hours, days, until they did. What other choice did I have?

With one final glance at the empty house, I stepped out and locked the door behind me. My vision was clouded with tears as I waited for the elevator, my body numb, my heart shattered beyond repair. He didn't just leave… he took the part of me that knew how to feel alive.

The elevator doors slid open, and I dragged myself inside, heaving a broken sigh. Just as they began to close, I saw him.

CJ.

He had just stepped out of the second elevator, his face a mirror of my own… tear-streaked and horrified.

For a brief second, our eyes met. A silent scream echoed between us, but before I could react, the doors shut, sealing me inside.

By the time I reached the ground floor and stepped out, I had barely managed to wipe my tears away when I felt a presence beside me.

He was there.

There were a million unsaid words lingering between us, written across his face, but he didn't speak them.

Instead, he moved closer, his steps deliberate, his gaze unyielding. My feet faltered, retreating instinctively. Slowly, I walked back into the elevator, with him pressing against me, my suitcase dragging in his hands.

The elevator closed, the silence between us thick with emotions neither of us could name.

Back in the apartment, he set my bag down and walked away without a word.

I stood frozen in place, my fingers trembling as I clutched the fabric of my dress. And then, before I could stop myself, I rushed into the bathroom, locking the door behind me.

He was back.

That was the only thought running through my mind as I slid to the floor, burying my face in my hands, sobbing harder than ever before.

A soft knock on the door made me jump.

I wiped my face, but it was pointless. My eyes were swollen, my cheeks red, my heart still bleeding.

I opened the door hesitantly.

"Sorry," he whispered, his voice hoarse.

"For what?" I choked out. "I am sorry for keeping the truth from you," I croaked as I sank onto the toilet seat, my hands gripping the edge. "I had no right to keep you in the dark. You have every right to hate me. To leave. To never want to see me again."

He frowned, confusion flickering across his face.

"What happened, not your fault," he said in his broken English. "Not at all. Stupid to think, why you sorry?"

"I…" My voice broke. "I should go."

"Are you crazy?" he hissed, his hands balling into fists. "You not going. Staying here. Always."

"What?" I whispered.

"Talk tomorrow," he murmured. "Sorry, I left."

He stepped closer, his gaze filled with something I couldn't quite name.

"Come to bed," he insisted, his tone softer now. But when I didn't move, he sighed and reached for my arm, pulling me up gently. "I am leaving you not," he whispered, his voice cracking slightly on the last word.

For a second, my heart stopped. But then it started again, racing wildly when he added, 'Not.'

"You really need to learn English," I whispered, a small, broken smile curling at my lips.

"I know," he admitted. "I will."

For the first time in what felt like forever, he smiled.

It was faint, hesitant, but it was there. And in that moment, I realized how much I had missed it.

"I think it's been a while since we…" he trailed off, his eyes darting toward the shower.

"We had sex yesterday," I snorted, despite myself.

"Yes. Yesterday. That was very far," he smirked, tugging at my shirt. "And you know me, I love sex with you."

A watery chuckle escaped me, but it quickly turned into a sob as I fell into his arms, the weight of everything crashing down once again.

"We have cried enough," he whispered, pressing a kiss to my hair. "You have enough, okay?"

I nodded against his chest, my fingers clutching his shirt like a lifeline.

"Now, I want smile," he insisted, dragging me toward the shower. Before I could protest, he turned the water on, fully clothed, and let the cold spray drench us both.

And then, as he looked at me, eyes dark with longing, he whispered, "Now, be mine."

And I let him pull me in, drowning in his warmth, his presence, his love.

40

Saranghae!

The day of my departure arrived, heavy with unspoken words and emotions neither of us were ready to face. The air between us was thick, not with hesitation but with the quiet acknowledgment of what was about to happen. He hadn't told me where he had disappeared to that night he left me alone, and I hadn't asked. Some things were better left unknown.

Before heading to the airport, I met Jay and his mother one last time. Both of them, without hesitation, insisted that I come back to CJ. "He loves you," his mother said with a knowing smile. Jay echoed her words, nodding firmly, as if my return was inevitable.

"Weird," I mumbled, chuckling bitterly. "He never told me that himself."

Jay gave me a pointed look. "Some people love in ways that don't involve words. Just look at everything he has done for you."

I didn't argue, because I knew he was right.

The afternoon before my flight, CJ took me shopping, insisting on picking out gifts for Dhriti and my kids back home. I watched as he carefully chose each item, thinking about what they would like, considering every detail. He even asked me about their favourite colours, their favourite snacks, their hobbies.

It was overwhelming… the depth of his care.

When I asked him why he was doing all this, he simply handed me his tablet. The words on the screen made my chest tightened with emotion:

"You are coming back with them, one way or another, so I have to make sure they like me, don't I?"

I didn't respond. There was no point in arguing when my own heart desperately wished his words could be true.

Then CJ drove me to the airport. The ride was silent, save for the occasional sighs we both let out. The city outside blurred as I stared out of the window, memorizing every street, every corner of the life I had built here. The life that now, I was leaving behind.

But he was different today.

There were no lingering touches, no desperate kisses, no hushed words of pleading. Just quiet acceptance. He walked with me to the check-in counter, carried my bag like always, and stood beside me as the final boarding call echoed through the terminal.

My heart was hammering inside my chest. This was it.

"CJ!" I called as the passengers began forming a line. He turned toward me, waiting. His dark eyes, filled with emotions I couldn't decipher, held me in place.

I took a deep breath, my hands trembling as I finally let the words slip past my lips.

"Nan neoreul saranghae."

I love you.

For a moment, time stood still. And then, his entire face lit up in a way I had never seen before. A grin, wide and beautiful, spread across his lips before he closed the distance between us in a heartbeat. His hands cupped my face as he kissed me… desperately, fervently, as if trying to etch the memory of this moment into our souls.

When he finally pulled away, he pressed his forehead against mine and whispered, "I love you too… and so much more."

Tears blurred my vision, but I smiled, because at least now, I had something real to take with me.

"And this is not the end," he insisted. "We will be together."

His English was… clearer than before. Better.

Noticing my surprise, he grinned sheepishly. "Taking English lessons, since living with you," he admitted. "Getting better, isn't it?"

"Very," I whispered through my tears. I didn't know whether to laugh or cry.

CJ took my hand and pressed it against his chest, over his heart. "I am letting you go today because I know even fate will get tired of keeping us apart…"

My jaw dropped at his poetic words, but his words didn't stem the flow of my tears…

He sighed and added, "We will be together," he promised. "I will come to you."

I wanted to believe him. I wanted to hold on to every word, every promise… but reality had a cruel way of making dreams feel impossible, of slowly pulling me back to a truth

I wasn't ready to face. And somewhere deep down, I knew I would keep bleeding his memories, because my heart wouldn't understand he was already gone from my life.

The final boarding call rang again. The air hostess walked over, politely reminding me that it was time to go.

I turned back to him, gripping his hand tightly, memorizing his face one last time.

"Oh, I will miss you so much," I whispered.

CJ exhaled sharply and pulled me into one last embrace, his hold firm, his warmth enveloping me entirely.

"We will be together," he murmured against my hair. "I promise."

And then, before I could say another word, before my resolve could shatter completely, I let go.

I walked toward the gate, feeling his eyes on my back with every step. And just before I stepped onto the plane, I glanced over my shoulder one last time.

There he was.

Watching… Waiting… Believing…

And I saw it in his eyes, how badly I was hurting him. Because I knew the worst kind of goodbye is the one that keeps echoing, long after the person is gone. And that's the kind this was… it will echo in our hearts forever.

As the doors closed between us, I held onto the only thing keeping me from breaking apart completely: hope. Because when something is real, truly real… it doesn't disappear, it waits, somewhere between memory and hope.

And I hoped this wasn't goodbye. Even though I once believed ours was a love that could never last, a part of me was beginning to believe otherwise.

Because love, real love, has a way of finding its way back, no matter the distance, no matter the odds.

And maybe, just maybe, ours will too.

Acknowledgement

Writing this book has been a journey of passion, made possible by the love and support of my wonderful readers. Your encouragement inspires me to keep exploring new stories, and it is because of you that this book exists. I hope it captivates you as much as my earlier works.

To my beloved husband, **Rajat Sharma**, thank you for your unwavering love, patience, and support. Your belief in me fuels my dreams, and I couldn't have done this without you.

To my wonderful kids, **Vihaan and Vanya**, for letting me steal moments to write, even when I should have been playing with you. Someday, when you read this book, I hope it makes you smile.

To my adorable nephews, **Dwij and Aadit**, your infectious laughter and sparkling eyes bring me endless joy.

To my entire family, who has always stood by me, encouraged me, and shaped me into the person I am today – your love is my greatest strength.

To **Anuj Kumar**, my publisher and a true friend, thank you for your constant support and for believing in this book as much as I do. Your encouragement means the world.

To my editor and friend, **Priyanka Lal,** whose suggestions helped me enrich the story further.

And above all, my heartfelt gratitude to the Almighty for guiding my path, blessing me with this journey, and giving me the words to tell this story.

With love and gratitude,
Your author,
Kritika Sharma

From Meera:

Hearts don't forget what they once called home…
No matter how far they wander.

From CJ:

I still find you in the quietest parts of my day…
and somehow, that feels like both a loss and a promise.

For You:

Some love stories don't need labels, don't need rules,
they live in quiet silences, where fierce hearts turn to fools.
And I hope you, my reader, find a love that stays,
a love that's soft and certain… forever yours, always.

Meera's and CJ's story
to continue
in Part 2 of
'Language of Love' series.